A MOTHER'S LOVE

A STORY BY LILLY BUCHANAN

1987
A mothers love
Lilly Buchanan

A MOTHER'S LOVE

First edition. September 4, 2024.

ISBN: 979-8227692191

Written by Lilly Buchanan.

To my Brandon, I love you so much Son. You will always be a prince to me. Love Mama

Dedicated to Brandon Keith. You will always be a Prince to me Son. Love Mama

Anna was a young girl who longed to be free from her mother. She got a job at a convenience store when she was seventeen years old. She became a single mother. She was madly in love but her crush only wanted her for sex. He specifically said, "If you won't, I have someone else who will." She didn't want to lose him. It would be 9 months before she learned, sex or babies don't keep a boy who is masquerading as a man.

She quit school in the 12th grade because she was pregnant with her first child. She had severe morning sickness and was so tired. She did not know she was anemic. Everyone she knew except her grandmother, kept telling her that her life was ruined, that she would never amount to anything. Her mother even tried to trick her into giving up her child for adoption, but she did not listen. Anna got a job at a convenience store but finding babysitters was difficult. Once she even took the baby to work with her. Her boss threw a fit, but she convinced him it was just until the babysitter could come to pick the baby up. It was a lie, there was no one to watch the baby. The baby boy ended up staying the entire shift, the boss never found out. If he did know, he never said anything. A convenience store is a good place to meet men of all kinds. Many of them are nice, they flirt with you and a lot ask you out. "You have to let them down easily if you don't want to date them." Her coworker Mrs. Tolbert told her. Anna told them all, she had a boyfriend, hoping her son's father would come to his senses and come back to them and be a family. She called the baby's father's mother to try to reason with her. The woman coldly said, "If I find out that baby is my son's I will take you to court and take him away from you and make sure you never see him again. I understand that you are a whore and your mother is a drunk. You must be so proud of your completely dysfunctional family."

Anna hung up on the woman and never approached her again. She wasn't a whore. She was a terrified, eighteen-year-old girl. Two months after that conversation, she received a telephone call from the baby's father asking her to come to his mother's house where he lived.

"We all have to talk to you about something," he said in a sweet voice. Anna said, "Okay, yes, I will be there in a few minutes."She borrowed her coworker's car and drove over to his house. When she arrived, she found it odd that no cars were in the driveway. The house was empty. She looked in every window...the entire house was empty. Finally, she asked a neighbor who was watching her look into the windows. "Where is the family that lived here?" "Oh, they all moved to Atlanta about a month ago." The neighbor said. Anna's heart broke. She had hoped he was calling her to talk about them being a family. They had moved to Atlanta which was one hundred and twenty miles away. He had sent her a message while pulling a prank in the process. She drove back to her job and tried to compose herself. She did not tell anyone in her family, because they would only say, "I told you so." Later that night at work, the boss gave her, a W40. Not knowing what it was, he told her to go to someone who prepares taxes and that she would get money back for the taxes they took out of her paycheck during the year. Her first year with a job. She went to a famous tax prepare and was given a check for $800.00 (eight hundred dollars). She cashed the check and was so excited. She went home to show her mother. "I can get the baby and me an apartment now and maybe a down payment on a car." She said excitedly. Her mother said, "Listen. The Navy was not able to pay my husband. He won't get paid for another week. Can you give us that money and in 7 days we will give it right back? We have helped you out; can you do this for us?" Anna said, "Sure Mom. I appreciate you letting us stay here. I will be looking at apartments for next week."

That evening when her mom's husband came in, Anna was playing with the baby and she mentioned her tax return to her mother's new husband. "I'm so excited, the baby and I can get an apartment and maybe put a down payment on a car. And let you two love birds have your space." "Yall aren't bothering us. We love having you all here. Did they say when you would get your check?" "Thanks. Oh, they gave it to me today! I cashed it. I'm so excited. And I want to say, I think it stinks how the Navy didn't pay you this month. That's so wrong. You go to work every day that's not fair." "What in the world are you talking about Anna?" he said, putting down Chance. Anna looked shocked, "I'm sorry, I didn't mean to get in your business. My mom asked for my tax return, all eight hundred dollars. She said the Navy didn't pay you, that you would be paid next week and y'all would give it back to me then." The husband became enraged. "That's a damn lie. I got paid." He screamed for Anna's mother to come to the room. "Rita, get in here NOW! "She came in, acting innocent, "Honey what are you screaming about? What in the world is wrong?" "You took Anna's tax return money! Give it back to her now. Every single dime, right NOW!" Anna's mother suddenly looked like a demon, 'That is a lie from the pit of hell. I never took anything from her. As a matter of fact. I gave her $20.00 today because she begged me for it. Anna, why are you trying to cause trouble with me and my husband? I want you to get your shit and get out of my house." Anna screamed, "Mom, I gave you all of my tax return money, all eight hundred dollars, you said Mike was not paid by the NAVY and would be paid next week, you said y'all would give it back next week." At that point, Anna's mother flipped out, she jumped at her, nearly hitting the baby. She grabbed Anna by her hair and dragged her towards the door attempting to throw her out of the house. "You are a filthy liar and I want you out of my house, now!" Anna's mother's husband forcefully got her off of Anna and forced her mother

into their bedroom. He screamed, "I swear to God, if you come out of our bedroom, I'm leaving you." Her mother continued to break things and curse Anna but she stayed in the bedroom. Her mother's husband took three hundred dollars out of his wallet and gave it to Anna. He helped her pack up her and the baby's things and drove her to a motel, which he paid for. "I will be able to give you the other five hundred on Monday when the bank opens. I am so sorry your mother did this to you. I was warned she was a thief and a liar; I am seeing it first-hand now. Our marriage is not going to survive. Your mother is an alcoholic and a maniac. I can't handle her anymore." "I'm sorry. I hope your marriage falling apart isn't my fault." "No, absolutely it is not. Your mother has a split personality, maybe even multiple personalities. I don't know. Sometimes she is wonderful, sometimes she is the devil's daughter. I can't live like this. I have asked the Navy to transfer me North so I can get away from her." "Thank you for giving us the money back. I will use it to make sure Chance and I stay away from her."

Mike said, "It is a crying shame what she did to you. Your own mother. And look Chance has a scratch on his left cheek. It must have happened when she jumped on you. I am so sorry Anna. You are a good mama. If you need anything please let me know and I will help you." He hugged Chance goodbye and then handed him back to Anna. Anna called work and told her boss that she couldn't come in. He told her that Mrs. Tolbert had retired; to call her and see if she was interested in babysitting. He knew the absence of a babysitter would be the only reason Anna wouldn't come in. She immediately called Mrs. Tolbert and she gladly agreed to keep Chance. Anna called her boss back and told him she would be in after all. Mrs. Tolbert had worked with Anna for almost a year and was crazy about Chance. The arrangement worked out great. Chance was a very happy child and he loved Mrs. Tolbert.

With the money Anna's mother's husband had given back to her, she was able to secure an apartment near her job, which was also close to Mrs. Tolbert. Anna worked for another 6 months before she was given a tip about a car and was able to purchase it. She was so thankful because she would no longer have to hire taxi cabs or bum a ride. It was such a relief. One of her customers bought her a car seat

for Chance. They were like that, good decent people. They brought clothes and

shoes his size, and greeting cards with cash for holidays and birthdays. Anna made a lot of friends in the short time she had worked there.

Four years later, on August 17, Jason Whitley, her manager called her into his

office. She was a little worried that something was wrong. He never called her into

his office.

"Anna, I am going to retire on the first of the year. I have been talking it over

with corporate and we want you to take over as store manager. You are honest. You

correctly handle conflict. It will be a lot more money and health insurance for you

and Chance. You will be on the day shift only unless there is an emergency.

I will personally train you. Please say you will take the position. Chance will go to

school soon, this way you can be home with him at night and on weekends. What do you say?"

"I would be proud to be the manager here sir," Anna said.

"Thank you so much, Anna. I know you will do a great job. That is why I

recommended you. Now, you will have to go to school on Saturday mornings for a

month or so to get your GED. The company will pay you to do that, and if you

decide to further your education the company will pay for that as well."

Anna was overwhelmed.

All she could manage to say was, "Thank you so much for this opportunity."

Everything went according to plan. Anna received her GED. It only took her one month of Saturdays before she took the test. She passed her GED on the first try.

She and Chance went every Saturday evening to visit her grandmother.

They all enjoyed that time together. They also spoke on the telephone daily. Anna learned from her grandmother that her mother's husband had kept his word and divorced her and moved away. She was not surprised to hear that her mother had remarried a couple of times since then. Her grandmother told her not to hate her mother because she had a mental illness that made her crazy. "We have to pray for and forgive the people who hurt us. That way God can forgive our trespasses. Unforgiveness does not hurt the other person, it only hurts us inside of our hearts. Nothing is worth that baby." Her grandmother was a wonderful woman. It was just hard to believe that was her mother's real mother. They were as different as night and day."

Anna tried to give her grandmother a little money and bring groceries to help her out the best she could. Anna and Chance were very sad when she passed away.

Anna went to the funeral home but did not attend the funeral to avoid her mother.

She did not want Chance around any drama. After the funeral, Anna's mother came to the convenience store and threw a fit, screaming and cursing, demanding to see Anna. Anna was not there, so the employees called the police. The officers knew Anna and called her at home. "What do you want us to do with this maniac?" Officer McGriff asked. "Just tell her to go away, or you will arrest her. Tell her she is barred from the store." Anna stated.

"Okay Anna, but if she comes back around, I am definitely locking her butt up. Let us know if you need anything." "I will Jacob, thank you!"

On Saturday, Anna took Chance to the park. They had a fun day playing on the swings, the slide, the merry-go-round, and the rocking horses. There were other children and their parents there, so it was a good experience for Chance. Anna was able to take a couple of pictures of him. He loved to make funny faces for the pictures. Anna had to beg him to look serious for a pictures. It made her laugh that he was so silly. For a second her heart hurt, he was growing up so fast. She wished she could have been a stay-at-home mom, but it just didn't work out that way. Her instant camera only took 6 pictures before it was full. She put it in her purse. She noticed a man with 2 small boys taking pictures of them and he had a beautiful professional looking camera. He looked Middle Eastern. He was very handsome. He caught her looking and smiled at her. They walked over to each other and introduced themselves.

"Hello, I'm Anna. That is my son, Chance on the swings."

The handsome man smiled and said, "Hello, I am Ephraim. I am here with my

brother's sons, Elihat and Josiah.

They came to visit me from where they live in Turkey. I am from Spain."

"Do you live here permanently?" Anna asked.

He smiled and said, "No I am attending University here."

"That's nice. Do you like it here in our city?"

He smiled again and said, "I like it better now."

Anna blushed and said, "Thank you. I was wondering if you would mind taking

some pictures of Chance. Sadly, my camera is out of film. I will pay you of

course."

Ephraim said, "It would be my honor to photograph Chance and you should take a

few with him as well."

While they watched the children play, they talked for a long time.

He was very easy to talk to. She didn't share any of her life, they just spoke of

world events and local news. He took a lot of pictures of the children, and some of

Anna with Chance. They all had a great time at the park. Ephraim suggested they

go eat lunch.

"Do you eat Spanish food? I know a great restaurant?"

"Yes, that would be great," Anna said. "Chance and I will follow you in our car."

Ephraim said, "That will be wonderful."

They gathered the children and headed towards the restaurant.

Anna was happy. Although this was not a date, this was the first time she had shown any interest in a man since Chance's father. Ephriam was tall and very handsome. He had long curly hair, beautiful dark brown eyes, a perfect light brown complexion, and beautiful teeth. He was not overly muscular but in great shape.

Anna wondered for a minute what he saw in her. She knew she wasn't a raving beauty, but he was attracted to her, she could see it in the way he looked at her.

The restaurant was very nice. Anna did not even know it existed. Ephriam ordered Paella for the entire table. It came in a huge pan and it was delicious. Chance was shy at first, but he gradually started to enjoy himself as the other children taught him to use the pita bread to scoop up the food. However, he dropped more than made to his mouth. The waitress finally brought Anna and Chance a fork and spoon. It was a great lunch.

For dessert, the waitress brought ice cream for the children and Flan for the adults. It was amazing. Anna was sad to see the afternoon end, but it was nap time for all the children. Ephriam asked for her telephone number and she was happy to give it to him. He gave her his number but assured her he would call her first.

That evening, Ephriam did call her after she got Chance down to sleep.

"Well, you are a man of your word," Anna said with a giggle.

"Yes, I am and I just wanted to tell you I had a great time today."

"Oh, I did too. Thank you again for lunch and a great time at the park. My son was

tired. I know he will sleep well tonight. He normally is very shy, but he had a great

time with your nephews. When are they going back home?"

"Sadly, my brother leaves tomorrow. They have been here for a week. They will be

on their way to Chicago to see our sister and her family then back to Turkey. I was

very happy to see them."

"I'm glad you were able to spend some time with them."

"Yes, me too. We try to see each other a couple of times a year."

"That's wonderful. I don't have any brothers or sisters. The only family I have is my grandmother, and a lady who keeps Chance for me, Mrs. Tolbert. Her husband passed away years ago and we kind of adopted each other. She is a wonderful lady and is like a mother to me and a second grandmother to Chance. I truly love her."

"Do you work?" he asked

"Yes, as a matter of fact, I just got a promotion, there is a convenience store, called

Seven Martins on Market Street. I started working there four years ago, almost five

years ago now. I started as a cashier. Recently I was promoted to store manager. It

will mean better money and benefits."

"Congratulations on your promotion. Have you celebrated yet?"

Anna giggled and said, "No I don't get out much."

"Well let me take you and Chance to dinner to celebrate please?"

"Okay, would Friday evening be, okay?" Ephriam said, "That would be perfect."

The next day after she took Chance to Mrs. Tolbert's and arrived at work, a delivery person arrived at the store with roses for her. The card said, "With much admiration, Ephriam."

Anna was blown away. She had never received roses before from a man and they were so beautiful. She grabbed the card and put it in her purse, away from prying eyes.

She began her first week of training with the boss to take over as manager. He teased her a little bit about the roses but didn't push her for the sender. She took them home the same day they arrived.

When Ephriam telephoned her that night she said, "I can't believe you sent me roses. No one has ever done that. They are so beautiful. Thank you so much. I wanted to call you but I was so busy with training."

"I knew you were busy. I am just happy you like them. How was the training?"

Anna sighed, "There is a lot to learn. I know I can do it, but I have to pay attention. I am writing a lot of things down so I don't forget. I am the youngest manager the chain of stores has on staff, so the pressure is on."

Ephriam said, "You are very intelligent and kind. I have no doubt you can master anything they present you with."

Anna smiled and said, "Thank you for believing in me. I don't have a huge support system. My boss is the one who recommended me for the position, and of course, I have my grandmother and Mrs. Tolbert. I want to give Chance a better life."

"I think you can do anything you put your mind to Anna."

"I certainly try. You know Ephriam, you never told me what you are studying in

school."

"I am learning to be an engineer. "

"Oh, my goodness. That is incredible. You must be very smart."

Ephriam laughed and said, "I don't know about that, but I am smart enough to

know a beautiful woman when I see one."

Anna said, "Oh...I?"

Ephriam said, "I'm speaking about you, Anna." Then he chuckled.

"I don't think I am beautiful, I'm okay." She said with a laugh.

"You are humble, that is an endearing quality you have. Your smile could light up

an entire city. Chance has your beautiful smile. He is a handsome boy who adores

you."

"He is my heart. I want so much for him to have a good childhood. Not like mine."

"We will discuss that another day, for now, we need to sleep. I will call you

tomorrow night. Is that okay?"

"Yes, thank you again. Sweet dreams."

"You as well my dear. Good night." For the next week, Anna learned her training very quickly. Her boss was extremely proud of her. She caught on very fast. Anna had no idea there was so much to running a store but it made sense. She had to know how much product they had and how much profit they were making. She learned how to make orders from different vendors, and she learned how to do payroll. When the regular customers found out she had been promoted, they flooded the store with balloons, and congratulations cards filled with money. They truly loved Anna and her child, they were so happy for her. Anna always made them feel loved. She celebrated them and it kept the public coming back to give her their business. She was a friendly, loving person.

Friday finally arrived and she and Chance dressed up for their date with Ephriam. Chance was sad that the other children had left to go visit their relatives but he was happy to be going out to eat and he liked Ephriam.

Ephriam picked them up in his sports car. It was very nice, a Camaro. He had bought a child car seat for Chance to sit in the back and be safe while he drove.

"Is seafood, okay?" he asked.

"Yes, that would be great," Anna said almost a little too excited.

Ephraim laughed because she covered her mouth in embarrassment.

"It's okay Anna. It's always okay to be excited and happy."

Chance laughed from the backseat and repeated to Ephraim, "Yes mama. It's okay to be happy." Then they all laughed.

The restaurant was a very fancy, expensive one. Anna had never been there. Ephriam carried Chance in on his shoulders and held Anna's arm as they walked in. The maître D made an odd face and asked if they had a reservation.

Ephriam said, "Yes, a party of 3 for Mohammad Ziel."

The Maître D checked his book, looked embarrassed, bowed, and then said, "Yes your Highness, right this way, please."

He escorted them to a table and pulled the chair out for Anna, then Ephraim, who let Chance off of his shoulder and placed him in the chair next to him.

The waiter came immediately and brought sparkling water and iced tea for everyone to drink. Then the waiter brought out a cake for Anna. She was surprised! She exclaimed, "Ephriam! You didn't have to do that, but the cake is gorgeous."

"I'm so happy you like it. I told the baker to prepare the prettiest cake she had ever made. I think she did an exceptional job too." She exclaimed, "Ephriam! You didn't have to do that, but the cake is gorgeous."

"I'm so happy you like it. I told the baker to prepare the prettiest cake she had ever made. I think she did an exceptional job too."

Chance said, "Whoa Mama. Is it your birthday?"

She giggled and said, "No son. I got a bigger job at work and we are celebrating."

Ephriam excused himself and came back with presents for Chance; a Tonka truck, and coloring books, with crayons. Chance was thrilled. He asked Anna, "Mama, is it my birthday?"

"No son, it is not your birthday. Mr. Ephriam is a kind man who loves to make us happy with his gifts. What do we say when someone does something nice for us?"

Chance held out his arms for a hug. Ephriam hugged him and Chance whispered, "Thank you, sir."

Anna put her hand over her mouth, this time to keep from crying. It touched her heart that her child was so precious and thankful.

They had a delicious dinner. Ephriam shared his food with Chance and let him try different seafood. Some of the things he liked, some he did not.

He loved the scallops, the shrimp, and the lobster but not the fish. Chance was so full he nearly fell asleep after dinner. Ephriam carried him to the car and by the time he put him in the car seat he was asleep. When they arrived at Anna's little house, he asked if he could carry Chance inside and she said yes. She carried the rest of the cake.

Anna showed him Chance's room and he took off his shoes, and Anna slipped on his pajamas and put him to bed. He whispered, "Mama get my truck and my coloring book, then let's say my prayers."

"Sweetheart, Mr. Ephriam has gone to get your things out of the car. We can say your prayers now."

He folded his hand and they both said, "Now I lay me down to sleep..." and Chance was asleep.

Anna finished the prayer, "I pray the Lord my soul to keep. If I should die before I wake, I pray the Lord my soul to take, Amen." She covered him up, kissed his little chubby cheek, turned on his night light, and turned off the overhead light.

Ephriam was waiting for her in the living room.

"May I stay a few minutes and visit with you?" he asked.

"Of course you may."

"You have a nice little house." "Thank you we just moved here. Our last apartment was even smaller. With the promotion, I was able to rent this place. It has all the space we need, plus the yard so Chance and I can play outside when he wants to. I have tried to make it pleasant for both of us. He loves to color and paint. I love to read, so I have designated areas for each of us. I am so proud of him. Chance had a great big heart full of love. He is a precious little boy. I am very blessed to have him.

"Well, I love it. You have made it a beautiful little home."

"I have done my best," Anna said with a forced smile. She wondered why he kept saying, 'little home.'

Ephraim said, "I have the pictures we took at the park. I hope you don't mind I had them put in a photo album. You can frame the ones you want. And also, I kept a couple of you and Chance. They were so beautiful."

They sat on the couch and went through the album. All the pictures were gorgeous.

"Ephriam are you a professional photographer?"

"No, my dear. The camera and the subjects, get all of the credit. Here these are the ones I kept of you and Chance. Aren't they delightful?"

Anna put her hand over her mouth, it was a stunning picture of her and her son.

"All of the pictures are wonderful. Thank you so much. I just can't thank you enough, but Ephriam, you don't have to buy us things to be in our life. We like you for being you. We have never had a lot of money so we are not used to going out to eat or having presents. Please don't feel like you have to buy us anything, okay? You are a wonderful man with a huge heart. I would want you in my life if you were God forbid... a homeless man."

Ephraim's eyes got big and he said, "God forbid!"

Anna could not stifle the laugh that was in her throat, "I'm trying to say, I would like you even if you didn't buy us anything."

Ephriam smiled and said, "I understand what you are saying, Anna. Now when can I see you again?"

"Well, I have training Monday through Friday for the next 5 weeks from 8 am to 4 pm. I am off on the weekends. So, my weekends are free. I take Chance to Sunday school on Sunday mornings from 9 am to 10 am then we come home. Other than that, we are free."

"Okay, can we go to lunch and then to the zoo tomorrow?" he asked hopefully.

"Yes, I think Chance will like that, I know I will."

He kissed both of her hands and said, "It's a date. I will pick you both up at 11:00. We will spend the day together. Good night my dear."

She smiled and said, "Good night. Thank you again."

He hesitated and said, "You do not have to thank me. It is my pleasure to get to know you and Chance."

Anna watched him walk to his car. He turned and looked at her for a minute then waved. She smiled and waved back and then shut the door. He made her feel so special but also scared. He was so easy to love. She felt it in her bones, in her dreams in her thoughts... She loved him. But could she move Chance to another country? Would they adapt to another culture? Would they be accepted in his world? If she was being true to herself, she wanted to keep Ephraim here and build a life with him and Chance here in the United States.

Anna didn't have anyone to talk to about this. No one had ever shown her the consideration, kindness, and generosity that this man had. She knew he was from another country and she knew the prejudices that the local rednecks she had met had for anyone they considered foreigners. She didn't see anything wrong with dating him.

He was wonderful. She prayed he was the person he seemed to be. No other man was being kind to her and her son. Taking her to dinner, sending roses, encouraging her, and giving gifts to Chance. He was so good with Chance. It made her heart flutter when she saw them together.

She read her Bible and she knew Jesus was from Bethlehem, He was not a white man like all these people thought he was.

She heard the Maître D, call him His Highness, was that a slight or an insult?

She had not told him that Chance was born out of wedlock. He may abandon her if he knew the truth. It was not Chance's fault that his father was a loser and a con man. Anna prayed until she fell asleep. She did not sleep well. She dreamed that Chance's grandmother stole him away from her. Chance woke her up and said, "Mama, you were crying in your sleep. Are you okay?"

"I'm so sorry son. I had a bad dream. Yes, I am okay. Do you want pancakes?"

He looked at her with suspicion but agreed to pancakes. He went into his room and colored in his coloring book. When breakfast was served, he showed her 3 pictures he had finished.

"Son they are wonderful. You did a great job. After we eat breakfast, I will show you some pictures Ephriam took of you and me at the park."

"Oh okay. I like him a lot mama. He is my friend and he is nice."

"Yes, he is a good friend to both of us sweetheart," Anna said with a smile.

Chance tried to cut up his pancake but ended up asking for help. "Son it is okay to ask for help sometimes. You will be big enough next year to cut up your pancake when you go to school next year."

"I hope so." He said with a worried look.

She mussed his hair and said, "Trust me it will happen. All good things happen in time."

Anna hoped that applied to her as well.

After breakfast, they looked at the photographs and Chance was very impressed.

"We look good Mama."

"Yes, son the pictures are great. You are very handsome and Ephriam is a great photographer too."

Ephriam picked them up at 11 and as they drove to the Zoo, Chance said, "Mr. Efman, My mama said you are handsome and I am a good photogrerpher."

Anna spoke up, "Chance, I said you are very handsome in the pictures and Mr. Ephriam is a great photographer." Ephriam laughed and said, "It's okay buddy. I think you both are right. You and I both can be handsome. I will teach you how to take pictures. How about that?"

Chance squealed with happiness. "I would really like to take pictures. Mama, I would take 100 pictures of you and they would all be so pretty."

Anna reached back and patted his leg, "I know you will be great at anything you do Chance." Ephraim winked at her and smiled.

Once at the Zoo, Ephraim took out a small camera and gave it to Chance.

"Now you have your own camera. I will teach you how to use it."

Chance was beaming. He was so excited, and said, "Thank you!"

He held Ephriam's hand the entire time. As promised Ephraim showed him how to use the camera. Chance was over the moon. He photographed many of the animals all by himself.

They all had a fun day. Chance was a little intimidated by the tigers and bears, and hid behind Ephraim's legs, but Ephriam explained that they were safe because the animals were caged and unable to get out to harm them. Ephriam took a lot of pictures too and he even asked the zoo staff to take pictures of the 3 of them together. It was a lovely time.

Ephriam asked Chance to pick out his favorite stuffed animal in the gift shop. He chose a giraffe and he loved it. They went to lunch at a Mexican restaurant. Chance had a great time and laughed when Ephriam played with him.

He was no longer acting shy; he was enjoying Ephraim's company and this made Anna feel happy. Chance had not been around very many men.

"I noticed you have a DVD recorder and player at your home. Is it okay if I bring 2 movies and go back to your house and watch it?" Ephriam asked. "I didn't want you to feel pressure to go to my place. If you don't feel comfortable, I understand."

Anna smiled at him and said, "Yes, that will be fine. Chance will need a nap by the time we get there. And just so you know, no funny business."

Ephriam laughed out loud and said, "Yes ma'am, I wouldn't dare."

Chance was asleep by the time he started the car. They held hands as Ephriam drove to her house.

Ephriam carried Chance to his bed and took off his shoes. Anna watched how tender he was with her son. Her eyes swelled with tears. She turned and went into the bathroom to wipe her face.

Ephriam went into the living room and put the movie in. He didn't start it until she came into the room.

He looked concerned when he saw her red eyes.

"Have you been crying?" he asked. He reached for her and she started crying again. "What is wrong? Tell me so I can fix it?"

She smiled and said, "Nothing is wrong. I am happy for the first time, except for of course the time with my child. "How long will you be here? What if we fall in love? I am so afraid."

He held her close, then kissed her passionately. "We have so much to talk about when the time is right. Right now, we are going to watch a movie and snuggle and maybe kiss. I promise I will answer all of your questions as I am sure you will answer mine. Everything will be okay."

He pulled her to the couch, into his arms and used the remote to turn on the DVD player. The movie was Casa Blanca, an old black and white movie, a love story. Anna cried at the end. Chance came into the room and asked why was Anna crying. She laughed and said, "It was the movie sweetheart. It had a sad ending."

Ephraim said, "I brought a happy movie for you, Chance. Are you ready to watch it?"

Chance didn't answer he just crawled up in Ephraim's lap and yawned. He motioned for Ephriam to lean down and he whispered in his ear. "Do you promise you didn't make my mama cry?"

Ephraim whispered back, "I promised. I would never make your mama sad on purpose. It was the movie."

Chance sat up and said, "Mama, do we have any popcorn?"

Anna said, "Yes, that is a good idea, Son, I will make some and get us some fresh tea."

The second movie was a Disney movie and all 3 of them enjoyed it. The best part was hearing Chance laugh. He had a deep laugh from his belly that was infectious. You had to laugh when he laughed. He managed to stay awake until the movie was over, then he hugged Ephraim and said, "Thank you for the movie. It was good. Not as good as the Zoo but it was good."

Ephraim told him he was very welcome. Anna ran Chance's bath, bathed him

then put him in his pajamas. He was very sleepy by then.

They said his prayers. He had started to include Ephriam in his prayers.

"God bless Mama, Mrs. Tolbert, and my friend Mr. Ephriam." And then he was asleep almost before his head hit the pillow.

Ephraim went into his room to tell him goodnight and he was hugging his stuffed

giraffe in his sleep. Ephriam kissed his forehead. He and Anna walked back into the living room. "I am so happy we have been able to spend this quality time together. I miss you when I don't see you."

Ephraim smiled and said, "I feel the same way. You are giving me heart trouble."

Anna looked concerned and said, "What do you mean? Are you sick?"

He put her hand on his chest near his heart, "Yes, I am sick. I am sick with love. I

dream of you at night. I can hardly wait to hear your voice on the telephone every

morning and night. I love your son. I feel like we are a family, or we can be."

He pulled Anna to him and held her. They sat on the couch. Ephraim looked

stricken. Anna asked, "How much time do we have before your studies are

complete?" He swallowed hard and said, "One year and 3 months."

"What are our options?"

"I have to go back to my father's land in Morocco after that time. You and Chance

can go back with me and we can marry. Would Chance's father object? You never

mention him."

Anna felt a panic in her heart. She stood up and paced back and forth for a few

minutes wringing her hands, trying to find the words. "I, uh, I was a 17-year-old

girl, I believed the lies of a 19-year-old boy who told me he loved me. He said we

were getting married so it was okay to have intimate relations. He kept saying he

would leave me if I didn't meet his needs. He kept saying a man has needs. He pressured me until I almost gave in, and then he forced himself on me. I thought I

was in love. I'm not sorry, because I wouldn't have Chance, however, I have had a

very difficult life. The young man ran away and abandoned us. He moved to

another city. He only saw Chance when we were at the same grocery store once

when Chance was 1 year old. He ran out of the store in fear. I can only assume, he

was running from the consequences of his actions."

She finally looked at Ephraim. He looked upset. He finally spoke.

"I would kill him with my bare hands for hurting you but I thank Allah that he is

not around to make your life terrible. He did you and I a favor by disappearing.

I would not have found you if he had stayed. I am in love with you, Anna.

I know for certain. We have one year and 3 months left to build a strong

relationship. My father is the King of Morocco, I am a Prince in his country. I am

required to go to my father when my education is complete but I need you and

Chance to go with me. Nothing else matters except you two are in my life."

Tears were flowing down his face. Anna went to him and they held each other.

She asked, "Is there more?" he nodded yes but said, "It will wait for another time. I

am so emotional right now I am afraid I may scare you away. I promised Chance tonight, I would not make his mama cry. I only want you to cry happy tears." He

started to kiss her tears away. Then they kissed passionately. Anna could tell he was reluctant to leave, but he was too much of a gentleman to ask to stay. She was both relieved and disappointed. She stood at the door watching him drive away then she went and took her shower. Anna wondered if she was making a mistake by getting attached to Ephriam, not knowing what the future held. He called her when he got home and simply said, "I love you, Anna, goodnight." She prayed before bed, then slept peacefully.

The next 8 months were blissful. Unless she was working or Ephriam was in

school, they were all together. Chance started kindergarten. He was painfully shy

and the teacher, Mrs. Mills assured his mother he would feel more secure as the

year went on. For the next 2 mornings, Anna lingered like a spy watching Chance

from the door window, making sure Chance was okay. Finally, the teacher came out to the hall and asked her to leave and trust the process. Ephraim worked with Chance on his at home work. He was a great teacher. Chance did become braver and started enjoying school. Anna made a point of putting Chance's artwork and school-graded papers on the refrigerator.

Ephraim bought a 3-ring binder to put some of the work to make room for more

papers. They let Chance decide each week, which ones stayed on the refrigerator

and which ones went into the binder. He loved that his mother and Ephriam

treasured his artwork. In Chance's 6th month of school, Ephriam came to talk to Anna and Chance, "I have something important to tell you. My father is ill and my brothers and I need to go and see him. I will return to you as soon as he is better. I will call you every night. I love both of you so very much."

He looked stricken. Anna could tell he was worried sick about his father and about leaving them.

Chance burst into tears, "I will miss you. Please come back."

Anna was brave but inside she was devastated. "We will pray for your father, that

he gets well soon. Is there anything I can do to help you?"

Ephraim cupped her face in his hands and said, "Keep praying and please wait for

me." Anna said, "Yes, I will wait for you, my love."

Ephraim kissed her forehead. "I will pay my rent and utilities ahead for the next 3

months. I should be back before then. If something happens and I am not back by

then, I will send you instructions. I am meeting with my advisor at school to let

him know I need the next semester off because of a family emergency. May I park

my car here so it will not be harmed in my absence?"

Anna said, "Of course you can, yes. I will make sure nothing happens to it."

Chance ran to his room and slammed the door. They could hear him crying."

"You better go talk to him Ephraim," Anna said quietly.

Ephraim was very sweet with Chance and explained why he had to leave. Chance

understood but said, "I know you need to see your daddy, but I will miss you."

"I will miss you and your mommy so much, Chance. You will be the man of the house until I come back. That means you have to take care of your Mama for me."

Chance said, "Yes sir, I will. Do you really love my Mama?"

Ephraim looked in his little eyes and said, "I love both of you with all of my

heart. You are my son." Chance said, "Yes sir, and you are my daddy. We love you too."

Ephraim asked Anna if she could get Mrs. Tolbert to watch Chance for a few

hours in the evening. She called and Mrs. Tolbert said, "Of course I will honey

bring him over when you are ready."

Ephraim said he would be back by 4 o'clock to pick her up.

As usual, he was punctual. He drove into the driveway at exactly 4 pm. He had a

bouquet of beautiful roses in a glass vase.

"Oh, sweetheart! They are beautiful. Thank you so much."

Ephraim swallowed hard, fighting back tears, and said, "You are welcome. If I had

my way I would plant you a million rose gardens so you would have roses every

day my love."

He kissed her, then said, "Come on baby, we are going to dinner."

Ephraim had found a new Indian restaurant in the next town over. The food was

delicious but knowing what they were facing made Anna feel sick. After

dinner, Anna went to the ladies' room to freshen up her makeup. When she came

back to the dining room, it was filled with balloons. She assumed it was someone's birthday but when she got to their table, she saw Ephraim is down on one knee.

Anna gasped as she realized he was proposing to her. He was holding a stunning

diamond ring. "Love of my life will you marry me?"

She was shocked but was able to say, "Yes, yes, I will."

Ephraim put the ring on her left hand, and gold bracelets on her right hand as the

rest of the customers and staff cheered. He kissed her forehead, her cheeks, her

chin, and her nose.

He whispered to her, "I will kiss your mouth when we get home."

They left and went to his apartment, where they made love for the first time. It was

magical. Anna and Ephraim both cried. He wiped her tears away and told her, "I

love you so much Anna, you have no idea how much."

"We love you too Ephraim. We have to tell Chance we are engaged."

"Too late mama, I asked his permission when we were in his room today."

Anna was shocked. She giggled, and said, "You boys are mischievous."

After a few minutes, Ephraim got up and said, "Come on sweetheart. I need to

show you some important things."

Once dressed and in the living room, he showed her a list. It had his private

telephone number in Morocco, his address there, there was a key to his apartment,

and the title and keys to his car. He had signed the title over to her.

There was also a key to a storage shed that he rented at the Livingston storage

facility, and one additional key for a safe he had in his closet.

There was a Power of Attorney letter he already had notarized leaving everything

in Anna's full care. He asked her to sign it. His banking information and

permission for her to withdraw all of the money and close the account if need be.

He also included the name of his counselor at the university in case he was

detained for longer than 3 months. He placed everything in a large manilla

envelope and handed it to her. Ephriam did not look into her eyes, he was scared of

what he would see looking back.

"I would like to bring the safe over to your house if you don't mind."

"Of course, that is fine dear," Anna said softly, looking at the floor.

Ephraim finished packing his luggage. It crossed Anna's mind that he was

packing so many clothes to go to a country that wore long robes most of the time.

She tried to shake it from her mind. She also noticed he packed all of his framed

pictures of her and Chance. He caught her watching and said, "If there is anything

here in the apartment, you want, you are welcome to it babe. We are going to be

married so what is mine is yours."

She shook her head no but did not speak. This was feeling like goodbye.

"I think I need to go pick up Chance now."

"I understand honey, let's go now," Ephraim said as he scooped up the safe.

They picked up Chance and he was half asleep.

He yawned and asked, "Did you get gaged Mama?"

Anna giggled and said, "Yes baby boy, I did," She showed him her big and

beautiful ring.

He said, "It is so pretty, but I already seen it, Ephriam showed me." Then he started

snoring. Anna stood their looking at Chance, then she got down on her knees and

prayed. In a few minutes, she went into the living room to be with Ephraim.

"Do you want me to take you to the airport?" Anna asked.

"No sweetheart it will be hard enough to say goodbye as it is. I will stay tonight

here at your place, then call a cab in the morning, to take me to my apartment to

pick up my luggage. Anna, I need you to believe me when I tell you I love you and

Chance. I love my father too, and if it were not mandatory that I return, I would not ever go back. I would stay here with my little family."

They made love one more time. Anna cried herself to sleep.

When she woke up at 4:00 am, Ephraim was gone.

There was a note on her pillow that said,

"You have made me so happy. I love you so very much. Hopefully, I will be back very soon. Pray for me as I do you. Don't let Chance forget me. Without you, I'm not okay.

All of my love, Ephraim

Anna was devasted, he didn't wake her up before leaving. She guessed that he

was trying to spare them both an emotional departure. Anna went to check on

Chance. He was sleeping but laughing in his sleep. She kissed his forehead.

In the living room where she had all of the pictures of Ephraim, Chance, and

herself, she had a minor meltdown. Grabbing a picture of all of them, she sank into

the leather sofa. She had a feeling that Ephraim was not coming back.

She negotiated with God begging for his safe return to her and Chance. "Please

God, I will do anything you ask."

Ephraim had been gone for a month. Anna was torn up inside.

He had not contacted her as he promised. Chance had asked a lot of questions that

she didn't have answers to. Her nerves were so bad that she had to vomit. She had

gotten herself so upset that she couldn't hold the coffee down that she was

attempting to drink every morning. She put a cold washcloth on her forehead and

tried not to cry. Anna thanked God that today was Saturday, she was off work and Chance didn't have school. "At least if I have a stomach virus, I can be at home to recuperate."

Chance woke up around 830 am and asked for pancakes. Anna hugged him tight and said, "Go wash your face and brush your teeth. I will get the pancakes started." "Can we go to the park mama?" Chance asked. Anna said, "No son, it is going to rain. Look out the windows and see the dark clouds. Why don't you color me some pictures?" He sat on the couch and cried softly. She walked into the living room and asked,

"Did you hurt yourself, son?"

He shook his head no. "I just miss my daddy. He woke me up to tell me he loved me and told me to pray for him and to take care of you, mama." Chance started crying harder. Anna held him tight and told him everything would be okay. "But Mama what if he don't come back? He said 'You are my son and I love you. "Anna said, "If he doesn't come back, then you and I still have each other. But we have to give him some time to see if he comes back."

After they sat there for a few minutes, Anna said, "Do you want to go buy a new

toy? Or go to a movie?"

Chance laughed and said, "Yes ma'am, and yes ma'am."

Anna laughed and said, "I should have known the answers to those questions.

Let's get you dressed."

They went to the toy store; Dream Toys are here, and he picked out a remote-

controlled car. It was expensive but Anna didn't care. Then they went to see

the new Disney movie, 101 Dalmatians. Chance was upset the woman was mean to

the puppies. Afterward, they went to lunch at Chucky Cheesing. There they ate

pizza and drank soda. There were a lot of games for them to play. Chance told his

mama, "My eyes are trying to close mama. I think they need a nap."

Anna giggled and said, "Okay son, let's go home."

Chance slept all the way home. There were no messages on the answering

machine. Somehow Anna thought there would not be.

Sunday came and Anna took Chance to Sunday School and they stayed for

church. She prayed so hard for things to work out with Ephraim. "But God if it is

not your will. I have to accept it." Anna knew she was lying to God, she had never experienced this type of grief and she wanted Ephraim back to share her life with.

She was trying hard not to let Chance know how devastated she was. Another month went by and no word from Ephraim. Although she did not show it, Anna was devastated. Her nerves were so bad, that she kept throwing up. She had lost weight and looked stricken, even when she tried to smile. She kept working and carrying on her regular life with Chance, but her heart was broken. She began having panic attacks, lost more weight, and felt physically ill.

Mrs. Tolbert finally insisted that she go to the doctor for some nerve pills to help her deal with her anxiety. Doctor Amos was a very nice, professional man. He gave her a complete physical and then told her to get dressed.

Once in his office, he said, "Anna, you are suffering from anxiety but I cannot

give you any medication for it because you are pregnant. I will give you the name

of a wonderful Obstetrician. Her name is Macy Radcliff and she is amazing. You

will get along famously with her."

Anna held up her hand and said, "Wait! What did you say?"

The doctor gave her a small smile and said, "I said you are pregnant dear."

Anna had no tears. She was stunned. "I, uh, I wasn't expecting that. We, we uh

used protection. Are you sure its not a stomach virus. I hear its going around."

"No method of protection is 100% fail-proof Anna." The doctor said with a sigh.

"Thank you, doctor. I am in shock over this but thank you for the examination."

"You are welcome. And Anna, when there are children involved you must dig

deep and find the courage to go on. You look like hell. You have to pull yourself

together. There is always a better day coming."

"Yes sir. I believe that is true. I also have a 5-year-old son. I will pull through this."

When Anna got home, she checked the mail. It was the 10th day after the eighth week that Ephraim had been gone, and a letter from the Royal House of Morocco arrived. Anna held it for about 10 minutes before she opened it. It was postmarked for the week that Ephraim left. She sat down at the kitchen table. Her hands were shaking and her head swimming. She thought she might faint. She walked into the living room to look at the picture of her, Chance, and Ephraim. Anna read the note.

This letter is to announce that the Royal Prince Ephraim and his brother the Royal Prince Mohammad were both killed in an airplane crash on November 17, 1996. They were en route to see their father, the King. Their plane was shot down by rebels, there were no survivors. You may keep or dispose of any property left in your care. Abim Mohammad Terin, Secretary to the King

Anna read and reread the letter, the room started to spin and she fainted. Fortunately, she was near the sofa and landed there. When she came to, she put the letter on the fireplace mantle. She thought, "Maybe if I don't read it again, it won't be true. Oh God, how will I tell Chance?" Anna looked at the clock, it was almost time to pick up Chance. She drove over to the school.

The teacher gave her a piece of paper advertising T-Ball for the kindergartners. She asked Chance if he wanted to play. He smiled and said, "No ma'am. But if they teach how to draw better, I will like that."

Anna hugged him and fought back her tears. They went to Mrs. Tolbert's for dinner. As Chance played with his toys, Anna told Mrs. Tolbert everything. "It's like a fairy tale gone wrong. My first real romance and it ends this way. I don't understand." Mrs. Tolbert said, "It's not ending any kind of way if you are carrying his child. He left you the gift of life sweet girl. He will go on in the life of his child. Anna, you are not the same young girl as you were when Chance was born. You are a responsible adult woman. You are strong, loyal, and a great mother. You can raise this child as you continue to raise Chance. I will be here to help you, though we may have to hire additional help to care for the new baby. I'm getting older and not as strong as I used to be. However, as long as I have breath I will help you. You are the daughter I never had Anna and I love you for that." Anna was so stunned about being pregnant, that she couldn't cry. "Do you think Chance will be mad at me?" "Mercy no. He will be tickled to be a big brother." "I love Ephriam, Mom. I love him with a passion I have never felt." "I loved Mr. Tolbert exactly like that honey. Then after 40 years of marriage, he had the audacity to die in his sleep. It took years of being mad at him to finally forgive him." Anna smiled at Mrs. Tolbert, "I'm sorry, you have experienced death as well. I am being selfish." "No, you are not. I didn't have a child so I didn't have to explain the situation. Give Chance some time. He may quit asking about Ephraim in time. If not then you can just tell him that he had to work in his country and could not come back. It will hurt his feelings but not devastate him if he knows Ephraim passed away. Gradually take away the pictures of Ephraim.

In due time Chance will learn to not miss him. It took Anna about 2 weeks before she could go to Ephraim's apartment. She called the landlord and explained the situation, and then she hired a moving company to transport all the furniture to a storage shed. It was one of the hardest things she had ever had to do. She found a box of letters he had written to her and photos of all 3 of them. She did not read them but put them in her car to take them home. She stayed while a cleaning crew came in and cleaned the apartment. She managed to hold it together and not faint or die from grief. When she gave the landlord the keys, the landlord handed her a check for the deposit and returned 2 months' rent.

"I'm so sorry for your loss ma'am. He loved you. He told me about you and Chance."

Anna was taken aback that he had shared that information with the landlord. But she supposed when you are happy you want everyone to know. Anna picked up Chance from school and they went to Denny's to eat dinner. "Mama you look sad. Is something wrong?" "No baby. Mama is just tired. Work has been busy, but it is supposed to be busy. I've been looking for art classes for you and I found a lady that we can visit on Saturdays. She is a retired art teacher. I can bring a book and read it while she helps you with your art. Would you like that?"

Chance took a big sip of his drink and said, "Yes ma'am as long as you stay. I would like that, but what if Efraim comes back and we are not there?" Anna hugged him and said, "Everything will be okay son. "She smiled at Chance. He was such a treasure. She actually felt sorry for his biological father missing out on such a great kid. Anna was trying hard not to talk about Ephriam. She knew she should have a talk with Chance about him dying but she hadn't accepted it in her own heart yet. She just didn't think she could tell him.

A month later, her baby bump was showing. Chance said, "Mama you are getting fat." Anna said, "Sit down sweetheart. Listen I have something to tell you and I hope you will be happy. You are my big boy and I love you so much. Um, mama is going to have a baby. But you are still my number one. Do you understand?" Chance looked confused. "You mean you have a baby in your tummy?" "Yes, dear." "When can I hold it?" "In about 6 months." "But you will still love me and we will still do things together?" "Chance, I love both of you. You will be a big brother. You will have to show the baby how to do things. I will need your help to care for the baby."

"I don't know how to care for anything except my toys." Chance said sadly. Anna giggled and said, "We can do this together, remember we are a team." He hugged her and said, "I love you, mama. We make a great team. And my daddy Ephraim he is part of our team. We all make a great team don't me mama?" "Yes, we do son. And we always will. Now I have to tell you as the baby grows, mama's tummy will get bigger and bigger. It won't be long until you can feel the baby kick." "Just tell me when, mama. I want to feel the baby kick. Is it a baby boy?" "I don't know yet Chance." "Okay." He said, then he ran to his room to color.

The next day, Anna drove to the storage shed that Ephraim had left behind. She spoke to the manager and showed him her power of attorney. "I already know ma'am. Ephraim filled me in on all of this before he left. He paid in advance for one year, but if you decide to remove the contents, I will understand." "I will let you know," Anna said sadly. She wanted to open the shed, but her heart was too heavy. She left without looking inside.

Chance's art class was going very well. He learned a lot and his pictures were getting better and better. The art teacher told Anna that he was easy to teach and

that he was a natural. Anna asked her if she knew anyone that taught

photography to children. The art teacher recommended Ralph Flagg.

"He is a phenomenal photographer and he works with children too."

Anna got his number and called him. He agreed to meet with Anna and Chance on

Sunday evening.

Anna surprised Chance with a new camera and lots of film. He was excited.

"I can take pictures of our baby mama."

Yes, and we will all take pictures together when the baby arrives."

They met with Mr. Flagg and Chance showed him his book of pictures that he had taken. Mr. Flagg agreed to work with Chance on Friday evenings from 5 to 7 pm.

Anna made sure she had Chance there for his classes. She was his support system

and a darn good one. The classes lasted for 5 months, then Chance graduated from

the class with a certificate. They framed the certificate and put it in Chance's room

on his wall. He was proud of the accomplishment. He took many pictures of Anna

and the baby bump as it grew.

In her 7th month, Anna was not feeling well. She asked Mrs. Tolbert to pick up

Chance and care for him so he didn't get sick being around her. The doctor thought

she had caught a flu bug. Her head hurt, her stomach was messed up and she had

chills. While in bed, she reached for the box of letters, from under the bed that

Ephraim had written to her. Each one was more precious than the next. He

expressed his feelings so beautifully, they were so true and deep. Anna cried,

spilling her tears on some of the letters. He did love her with an unbridled passion.

One letter, he just kept writing her name over and over. Another had a poem he had written to her. He expressed how he begged Allah to let her say yes to his marriage

proposal and how he would spend the rest of his life making her and Chance happy

and safe. He expressed gratitude for finding her at this time in his life and having a

son. She cried more. This time she cried for Chance because he still did not know

Ephraim was dead. Anna got up out of bed and crawled to the bathroom. She

vomited violently, then sat on the cool bathroom floor. She washed her face and got

back in bed. She was putting the letters into the box when she noticed a torn-up

piece of paper. She pieced it together and saw that Ephraim had written a prayer to

Allah, his god. She felt awkward reading it because it was so personal. It was

almost like she was intruding. Guilt swept over her, yet she felt a pull towards the

torn paper and decided to read it. She didn't know why he hadn't thrown away the

torn paper. She noticed tear stains on the paper, and it felt like a punch to her heart.

They both were so in love, how could this happen?She read the letter addressed to

Ephraim's god, Allah.

"Allah please show me how to explain to Anna, the love of my life that I will be King when my father dies. She will be my Queen. Our beloved Chance will be a prince. How do I tell her that we will have to tell all of Morocco that Chance is her brother and not her son? Allah, I beseech you with every fiber of my body and soul, how do I make her understand that this is how it is done in my country?

I am so torn. I can't imagine the look on her face if I tell her this. Surely she will feel betrayed, and disappointed in me for even suggesting such a thing.

I wish death to me; instead of hurting or disappointing either of them. I love them so much. I have contacted my brothers, and they all say, this is the only way if I intend to marry her, and I do, I will. I need her forever in my life. I need Chance as my son. We are a family already. Allah, I beg you please make a way. Again, if you decide not to make a way, please sentence me to death. I cannot be without my loves. Amen"

Anna sat up in the bed. She was in a cold sweat, her heart pounding against her

chest and for a minute she was afraid she might die. Ephraim knew she would

never present Chance as her brother. That would have been the deal breaker and he

knew it.

She wondered if Ephraim had abandoned them because he knew she

would never agree to those terms. Maybe the note from the Royal Family was a lie,

maybe he wasn't dead. In any case, Chance was her priority, her lifeline, as the

new baby was as well. How sad, another father would miss out on raising his child.

Anna decided she would rather believe Ephraim was alive and leading his

country than believe he was dead.

After 3 nights and 2 days, she was feeling better and went to pick up Chance from school. He was very happy to see her, "Mama I missed you so much. Are you

better now?" "Yes sweetheart, I am better now. Have you had fun at Nana Tolbert's?" "Yes ma'am. The neighbor children, Vance and Keri came over and we played board games. Nana made us lunch, so we had a picnic. Then we watched Gunsmoke on television. I like Westerns."

"That sounds wonderful son. I'm glad you had fun."

They went and picked up burgers and fries and then headed home. After dinner

Chance read 2 books to his mama's stomach.

"I am reading to the baby so she will be smart."

Anna asked, "How do you know it's a she? We haven't found out if it is a boy or a

girl yet?"

"I have a secret. I want to tell you mama, but I don't want you to be sad."

"You can tell me anything, son."

Chance beamed, "I had a dream mama. Ephraim told me to watch over you and my

baby sister. He reminded me I was the man of the house. He also said he loved us

so much and to never forget that."

Anna nearly fainted but steadied herself against the wall. She grabbed Chance and

held him.

"Son we will get through this. Remember we are a team."

Two months later, Farah Lauren was born, 7lbs 3 ounces, 19 inches long. The

delivery was easier this time. She was a gorgeous baby and looked just like her

father with a head full of black curly hair and dark brown eyes.

Chance was mesmerized by her. He kept counting her fingers and toes.

"She's beautiful mama. Just like you."

Nana Tolbert told him to sit down, so he could hold his new sister. Chance was

smiling big and he carefully held her with Nana Tolbert's help. He whispered to

her, "I promised I would take care of you and Mama. I will. We are a team."

Years went by and Anna never married. She raised her children with the help of

Mrs. Tolbert until Mrs. Tolbert passed away when Farah was 9 years old, and

Chance was 14 years old.

The age of the internet had come upon Anna and she used the computers regularly

in her research while achieving her Master's Degree in Finance and Senior

Management. She had been promoted to Assistant General Manager.

They offered her the General Manager position, however, she turned it down

because she would have to move to a city up north, and she didn't want to do that

because the children were happy with their lives and their schools.

Chance was playing soccer and he was the official photographer of his high

school's yearbook. Farah was in the Choir and the Drama club at her elementary

school.

Anna was so happy that her children were well-adjusted and happy. She shared in their lives completely, even though she had hired a move-in housekeeper and cook.

There just wasn't enough time in the days to do laundry, cook a delicious dinner,

and clean the house like it should be.

Mrs. Everly was a widow and had no family in the area. Anna had hired her from

her resume on Redeem. A Christian organization that assisted people with securing

employment. She was a perfect fit for the family. The children adored her. She

even came to Farah's concerts and plays. Mrs. Everly was part of the family, an

important part.

Anna had purchased a gorgeous 6 bedroom, 3 bath home with her newfound

success. Of the extra 2 rooms, one was for Chance to use, it was a dark room to

develop his film, and the 2nd was a room that Farah used to make costumes and

props for the plays she was participating in.

The rest were bedrooms for everyone.

Once Anna graduated with her college degrees, she finally went to Ephraim's

storage shed. She had paid for it for years and never entered it. Anna picked a time

when the children were in school and gathered her courage.

Anna told the owner that she was going into the shed. He offered to go with her but

she declined his offer.

"I think this is something I have to do alone."

"Well, I am here if you need me."

Anna gave a half-hearted smile and said, "Thank you."

She parked her Audi in front of the shed. It was terrifying. She had no idea what

she would find inside the shed. It had sat dormant for over 7 years. As she put the

key in the lock, her heart was racing. She suddenly missed Ephraim so much.

She had an overwhelming desire to fall to the ground. After all of these years, she

and Chance still missed him. He didn't even know about Farah being born. She squared her shoulders and made herself open the shed.

She pulled the lock off and raised the metal door. The sun was shining so it took a

minute for her eyes to adjust. There was expensive furniture and beautiful framed art in the shed.

A gorgeous desk covered with dust was set up with a picture of Ephraim, Chance,

and her. Tears began flowing.

"I don't know if I am strong enough to do this." She said to God. She didn't

realize she had raised her fist to her mouth and was biting it to keep from calling

out for Ephraim.

There was a single piece of paper on the desk. It was a letter to his father.

Anna blew the dust off it and sat on a nearby dusty stool. "Another letter that I

don't know if I should read. I have invaded his privacy before and received

information that I did not want." She read the letter.

"My dearest Father, My King. I have no choice but to advocate my position as your successor. I cannot give up my new family. They need me and Allah knows I need

them. They are everything to me. I know you will be disappointed, perhaps even

angry. Please try to understand Father. I have never been in love. All the women

you and my brothers pushed towards me in the past and I did not have feelings for

any of them. I know you thought sending me away to university would help

change my mind, and see things your way. It did not. I would rather be poor,

penniless, but still have my little family here, rather than leave them. I love you

Father, and I have never defied you in my entire life, until now. I love her with a

passion I have never felt. She is my missing rib, that Allah took from me to make

my helpmate. She has a 6-year-old son; his name is Chance and we have bonded

as close as father and son. I plan to propose to her tonight. The thought of her

being my wife is the greatest feeling I have ever felt. I will adopt Chance as

my own. Father, I can't imagine how your heart is wrenched. My gut is wrenched

with having to disappoint you, but I must follow my heart. I will give up my

position for my brother to advance to the throne, and then I will bring my family

for you to meet when you like. If you choose not to meet them, I will honor your decision. However, I won't come without them. I love you, Father. I pray you will

receive this with the heart of a man. Not of a King. I know you have men you can

dispatch to bring me home. Please do not do that. Please let me live this life with

my new little family."

It was not signed. Anna was dumbstruck. He was at one time willing to give up

his place as King of Morocco, for her and Chance. Anna was stunned. After an

hour, she called a moving company and made an appointment for them to meet her

at the storage shed in 3 days. They transported all of the furniture and art to her

huge garage. She spotted an enormous package in the back of the shed. It was

wrapped and bound tightly. The movers carefully placed it in their truck.

Once everything was put into her garage, she paid the movers, and they left. The

children asked her about the furniture but she changed the subject. Anna didn't

think she could put the furniture in the house. It was just too painful of a memory.

She did put Ephraim's letter to his Father in her Bible.

The huge package was calling to her but it took months before she could open it.

The package contained packs and packs of money. United States monies. Anna

assumed it was how Ephraim financed his education and his lifestyle with her and

Chance. She taped it back up and draped a quilt around it then tied long twine and

ribbon around it. She didn't get excited, instead it upset her.

She would have gladly given all of that money to hold and kiss him one more time.

That night it came to her that she could use the money to pay for Chance and

Farah's college education if they chose to go to college. If not, it would buy them

cars and houses.

Anna waited until the children were asleep, then cried herself to sleep. The wine

did not help her rest. She still wore her engagement ring after all of these years and

all of the information that she received about Ephraim's death.

She reasoned with herself, 'That kind of love only comes along once.'

Many men still asked her for dates, but she would hold up her ring hand and say,

"Sorry, I'm spoken for."

She knew if was a defense mechanism, but she couldn't love anyone but Ephraim

and her family.

Anna was very glad she had her children and her work to keep her busy so she

didn't have many nights like this night. Feeling sad, and sorry for herself.

Chance came home from school and was sitting in the living room when Anna

came in from work. He looked like he had been crying. His eyes were red and puffy. Immediately Anna rushed to him and said, "Son what is wrong?"

"Mama, I need to talk to you. It's important."

Anna panicked. She thought maybe Chance had gotten into trouble.

"What is it son, you know you can tell me anything. We are a team, remember?"

"Um, this is hard." Tears stung his eyes. He wiped the tears away, but they kept flowing.

"Mr. Pickett, my history teacher gave us all an assignment. Ironically, when he

gave out the assignments... he chose Morocco for me to do my paper on."

Anna sat next to him and put her arm around him.

"Did it remind you of Ephraim, son? Is that why you are so upset?"

He shook his head no and handed her a stack of paper. The papers were printed out

from a computer in the library. The articles stated that King Ephraim had ruled

Morocco, since his father's death, and while he considered his country to be allied

with the United States, he vowed never to travel to the States again.

The many pictures clearly showed Ephraim as King. He was surrounded by his

five wives and 15 children. Ephraim looked old and miserable, in every single

picture. Many of the little girls looked like Farah. Anna was too stunned to be

upset. Her eyes kept returning Ephraim. He looked terrible and it hurt her to see.

Chance asked, "Mama, are you mad at me for telling you? I just could not keep this from you. We have waited all this time for him to come back to us. Poor

Farah doesn't even know her father."

For a few seconds, Anna could not speak. She was so happy he was alive, yet

gutted that she and her son had been forgotten. Anna pressed her lips together, then

said, "Sweetheart, you, Farah, and I are a team. We survived many heartbreaks and

troubled times, but we survived. I think we should put these papers in the safe.

Maybe when Farah is grown up she will want to see them. I will come to see Mr.

Pickett tomorrow and ask him to give you a different country to do a research

paper on. Everything will be okay. I promise."

Chance hugged her tight and sobbed, mourning Ephraim. He wept bitterly. Anna

was just about to fall apart when Farah came in from outside.

"What is wrong Chance?" she asked.

He wiped his tears with his shirt and said, "I just had a bad day sister. I will be

okay." He got up and went to his room. He continued to cry in his room. It made

Anna angry with Ephriam. Where was the love and protection he promised?

Anna did not sleep that night. She stayed up and looked at all of the papers she

had put in Ephraim's safe. She could tell he was angry and miserable. His eyes

looked fierce like he was in pain. He looked almost violent.

No smile was on his face. His hair was shorter, he was older. But there was no

denying it was him. Each beautiful wife looked unhappy and hesitant.

Anna prayed, "God, please help me to forgive whoever kept Ephraim from us.

I believe with all of my heart that he loved us. Please help Chance to heal from

this new information and help me too. I have never been more stunned in my life

than to see Ephriam alive, but it pains me to see him so miserable. Please give him

a feeling of peace, Your peace. One day I will have to explain all of this to Farah,

and on that day, I pray you will give me the right words. Please bless my little

family and give me the courage to continue to move forward. Amen"

Anna went out to her car and broke down. She had waited for this man for years,

never wanting to believe he was dead, never accepting the note that came stating

he was dead. He was always with her. Every time she looked at sweet Farah she

saw Ephraim in her face and eyes. Anna had never contacted Morocco about

Farah. Only Mrs. Tolbert knew who her father was in the royal family. Anna had

decided to not tell them in case they sent someone to take her away. Anna knew

she was capable of murder if someone took her children.

They may have taken Ephraim from her, but not her children. Terrible, debilitating

heart-wrenching, sobs came from the car. When she was able to get out of the car,

Chance was standing on the porch. His eyes wide and swollen from crying.

"Mama, are you okay?"

"I will be son. It's okay. Do you need to talk about this?"

"Yes ma'am. I just don't understand why this happened. I mean you got engaged

and everything. He was so good to us. What happened?"

"I have a feeling that when he was called back to Morocco, his father forced

him to stay. He had a duty to his country to be their King once his father passed

away. I believe he truly loved us, Chance. And I do not believe he had anything to

do with the announcement of his death. Ephraim would never cause us pain on

purpose. The royal family is powerful and they have to rule their country. I am so

sorry son that I was not with you when you found out the truth. Thank you so much

for letting me know. I would have wondered for the rest of my life if you hadn't

found those articles online. This somehow should give us closure. I will share this

information with Farah when she grows up."

"Don't tell her Mama. She doesn't need to hurt like we are hurting right now."

Anna hugged Chance. "I love you son. I am so proud of you."

Chance went to bed, and Anna found a rag and some furniture polish.

She went into the garage and polished Ephraim's furniture as she had for years. She

could never bring herself to bring it inside her home, but she thought maybe

Chance or Farah would want it one day. She had the garage set up like a living

room. No pictures of Chance, Ephraim, or herself, however, there were beautiful

pieces of art and the furniture was stunning.

Years ago, as her salary increased, she had the garage enclosed for air controlled

environment to keep the items from deteriorating. She had purchased sheds for the

backyard for Chance and Farah. He used his as a storage shed for his bikes, his 4-

wheeler, and tools. Farah decorated her shed as a private library. The library was

adorable, decorated in pink and white.

Mr. Prichett was understanding, when Anna asked him to change Chances country

due to private family business with the country. He changed Chances country to

Ireland, and did not give any other student Morocco.

One Saturday, Anna was in her office, looking at her engagement ring. She

promised herself she would not cry anymore. She was resolved that everything

happens for a reason and she realized that she must accept her fate. Her job was to run stores and to raise her children. So far, she was successful at both quests. The

six stores she was responsible for were wildly successful, and more importantly,

her children were great students and great people.

Many years ago, the university that Ephraim had attended sent her a posthumous

honorary degree in Ephraim's name to her address. It showed he was a graduate of

the Science of Engineering.

She had framed it and put it in her room. After Farah started kindergarten, she hid

it in her closet. After Farah learned to read, it went into the safe.

With this new information that Ephraim was alive, Anna decided to anonymously

mail the degree to the King of the Royal Family in Morocco. She did not put a

return address, and she decided to send it to the Royal Palace in Morocco. She had

typed all of that information on the manilla envelope.

The degree was the only thing in the envelope. As she handed the envelope to the

postal worker she suddenly wished she hadn't decided to do this. It may cause

Ephraim pain through his memories. She didn't want to devastate him as he had

her. She asked the worker for the envelope back. The postal worker asked, "Are

you sure? You have already paid for the postage."

She smiled a half-hearted smile and said, "I need to think about it some more."

Anna drove back home and put the envelope in the safe. She knew in her heart

that Ephraim would be so upset that she found out he was alive and, on the throne,

in his father's place. No sense in hurting him too. He looked so unhappy already.

When Chance turned 16 Anna took him to get his driver's license. He passed the

written test and the driving test on the first try. When they arrived back home, he

was presented with a Blue Chevrolet truck. It was his dream vehicle. It had the

type of cool wheels that he had talked so much about, and Anna had purchased the

tag, title, and insurance for Chance. She had used some of the money Ephraim had

left behind, and some of her own money. So technically it was a gift from both of them, but she didn't give Ephraim any credit. Chance was over the moon with

excitement. He kept saying, "Thank you so much, mama. It is just what I wanted.

Thank you!"

Anna was so happy to see Chance happy, and thankful for his gift. He had been

practicing his driving with Anna in the car. He was a careful and skilled driver.

Anna was so proud of him. Chance drove the truck to his buddy's house to show

him. Anna and Farah had accompanied him as his first passengers. They stopped at

a local restaurant where Chance's other friends were there to celebrate with him.

He was surprised to see all of his friends, and a birthday cake.

He was anxious to eat and get outside and show off his new truck.

Anna laughed. She assumed all of the parents from the private school her children

attended would call her and tell her thanks, now they had to give their own

children brand-new cars. It turns out, that those parents did call and all of their

boys wanted Chevrolet trucks.

Farah took dance classes and drama classes. She had many recitals and plays. Anna

and Chance attended all of them. She was such a sweet girl, and she always had

a positive attitude like her father did. As she grew older, she looked so much like

her father. Chance told his mother, í know she looks like Ephraim, but she is not

Ephraim she is our Farah and we have to remember that mama. We can't risk them

taking her away from us." Anna was shocked, "Son why would you say that?"

"At the recitals and plays, I have noticed muslin-looking men taking pictures and

taking notes. I didn't want to alarm you until I knew for sure. I followed one to the

men's room last night and confronted him. He laughed and said he had a niece in

the program but when pressed, he couldn't tell me her name. I don't know if

Ephraim would take her. I am not blaming him. Maybe it's a cultural thing mama

but we have to be careful."

Anna was shocked. Maybe Ephraim had been keeping an eye on them.

Maybe he guessed about Farah, or worse saw Anna when she was pregnant.

Anna tried to contain her emotions and not panic. She gave specific orders to the

housekeeper that no one was allowed in the house that was not family.

"Do not open the door to anyone unknown to this family, I mean no one."

The housekeeper said, "I promise."

Anna called a security company and had them install a top-of-the-line security

alarm in the house. She then had bars put on the window and front and back doors.

She gave the children keys and the alarm code. She also hired men to guard her

children in school and while she was at work. Anna left work early one day and

went to a pawn shop and bought 2 handguns and ammunition. The salesman gave

her the name of a police officer who taught firearms safety in his spare time. Anna

called him and they made an appointment to meet at the police department firing

range. Robert Ingles was a very nice man. He was very knowledgeable about guns

and after several months of lessons, Anna became a proficient marksman. She paid

Robert handsomely for his services. Robert encouraged her to enter a local women's shooting contest. She came in second overall. Anna was relieved she

could protect her family if need be. Robert was proud when she came in second in

the contest. He was there to cheer her on.

Robert asked her to dinner to celebrate. It took Anna by surprise, but she assumed

it was just a friendly request.

"Okay, but I want to bring my daughter if you don't mind."

He smiled sincerely and said, "That would be wonderful. I can tell you love your

children. I have a daughter, Dorothy, she is 13, I can bring her, and that way the

girls don't have to be bored with us old folks."

Anna said, "That would be wonderful. My daughter Farah is always making a good

friend."

"Is Saturday evening, okay?" he asked sheepishly.

"Yes, that will work. Oh, and Robert please don't bring me flowers."

He laughed and said, "Okay, can I bring you a tire?"

She laughed and said, "Wait, What?"

"Just kidding Anna." He said with a laugh.

As the week progressed, neither Anna nor Chance saw anyone following them, and

believe me, they were looking. Neither the cameras nor the security team saw

anyone either. This allowed them both to rest easier. Maybe it was someone else

they were looking for.

Saturday came and Anna found herself more than a little nervous. It had been years since she had gone to dinner with anyone other than her children. Chance

encouraged her to have a good time and to try and enjoy the dinner. Farah was

excited about meeting Robert's daughter, Dorothy. Anna made sure Farah

understood that even though the girls could have their own table, it had to be right

next to her so she could keep an eye out for them. Farah sighed but agreed.

Anna asked, "Why are you sighing Farah?"

"I just don't understand why we have so much security around for the last 3

months. Is something wrong? Has someone threatened us?"

Anna blushed and said, "Honey, I can't explain it right now but I will explain

everything to you soon." Farah shrugged her shoulders and went to get dressed.

Anna felt terrible. She should have tried to explain to Farah, but it was so deep and

sad. She didn't want to upset Farah. And she wasn't ready to relive everything.

Robert had picked a German restaurant. She was a little upset when she saw Robert

holding a small bouquet of flowers with him. She had specifically asked him not to

bring her flowers. Anna introduced Robert to Farah.

"It is very nice to meet you Farah. This is my daughter Dorothy."

The girls said hello to each other.

"Oh, and I got these for you, Farah," Robert said, as he presented her with the bouquet.

Farah was surprised. "Thank you, sir. This is my first-time receiving flowers. They

are so pretty."

Robert smiled and said, "You are very welcomed." Then he turned to Anna and

said, "I have ordered your tire ma'am."

Anna giggled.

Anna and Farah had never eaten at this German restaurant. It was a lot of fun.

They had a band; people were dancing and the food was delicious. Robert

explained the different types of dishes available and threatened to buy everything

on the menu if they didn't choose something. He explained that one of the dishes

was basically a huge pork chop, the other was sausage.

"Whatever you don't eat, you can take home for later. And don't let me forget to

get Chance something also." This touched Anna's heart that he was considerate of

her other child as well. Anna and Farah ordered the schnitzel and potatoes. Robert

also ordered a German potato salad was amazing.

"It's always good to try new things to eat, so you don't miss out something that is

delicious."

The girls felt like grown-ups at their own table. They giggled and talked constantly.

The manager put their sprite into wine glasses and that thrilled them. It felt so good

to see Farah enjoying her evening. She normally was quiet and reserved.

Robert and Anna did not have a very deep conversation. He whispered to her that

Dorothy's mother had left him for another man, and he fought for Dorothy and won

in court. "She was only 5 years old. Her mother never tried to visit her. We have

done great together. This is probably my 3rd date since I got custody of Dorothy."

"Well, you have me beat. I haven't dated anyone since Farah's father left. I just

keep busy with work and the children's activities.

Farah is in drama and dance and Chance is a soccer player and a photographer on

the High school yearbook. He loves photography. My home is like an art gallery.

He has such an eye for detail."

"Dorothy is in choir and gymnastics. She is extremely dedicated. Aren't we lucky

they didn't join the band?"

Anna laughed and said, "Oh my goodness, yes we are lucky."

Robert spoke about his work. "I was in patrol services for 5 years, then I was

promoted to the homicide division where I have remained for the last 10 years."

"Oh my, that must be trying on your patience and heart." "It is difficult seeing so

much death and destruction, but I approach it from a practical viewpoint and try to

avoid the emotional side. Don't let me mislead you, I still get upset when the scene

is overly graphic, but as the Captain, I have to keep it together and encourage my men not to get caught up in the emotional side. I always debrief them during any

death."

"That is good to know you care about your men. It is so important to have a good

working relationship with your team."

"I agree. Now your turn Anna." Robert said with a smile.

"Oh goodness, my career is nothing like yours. I am an assistant General Manager

of the (4) Seven Martin's convenience stores. It's the only job I have ever had.

I started when I was 17. I have been there for 13 years and worked my way up

from cashier to where I am now. It is stressful sometimes dealing with the

employees and the public. Somehow, I make it work. It's been good for my

children and me." "That is a great story," Robert said with a smile.

"Yes, rags to riches. I wrote that story." Anna said with a giggle. After dessert,

Robert said, "Anna, I know this is probably going to sound forward, but would you

consider another date, just you and I?" Anna felt terror in her heart, "I, um,

couldn't we do a few more with the children present? I am so scared Robert. I need

to be friends first, do you understand?" He put his hand on top of hers and said,

"Yes, I completely understand. We will take it slow, but I truly like you."

Anna blinked back tears and said, "I have grown to admire you on the shooting range. You are calm, confident, and considerate. I appreciate those qualities in

you." Robert said, "Well that is a start."

The waiter brought Chance's dinner, and they gathered the girls. They all hugged

in the parking lot. Robert kissed Anna's hand, and she swore she saw a flash of

light. She looked around but did not see anyone with a camera, however it was

dark outside.

"Is it okay if I call you tomorrow evening?" Robert asked.

"Yes, that will be fine. We will talk again soon. Goodnight."

Driving away, Farah was very excited about making a new friend and told her

mother all about Dorothy. "She is so nice mama, and she is in the Choir and

gymnastics. Isn't that great?" "Yes, honey. That is wonderful. Of course, I am

extremely proud of you and your brother's accomplishments too."

"It's crazy. She doesn't have a mother, and we don't have a father. I hope you and

Mr. Robert hit it off. You have been single all of my life mama. Don't you get

lonely sometimes?"

Anna wasn't ready for this very grownup conversation. She cleared her throat and

said, "Farah, I have you and Chance that give me great joy and a sense of worth. I

think that Mr. Robert and I could become great friends. But don't you girls try to

marry us off to each other. I am content with my life as it is."

Farah said, "But Chance and I won't always be here mama. What will you do then?"

Anna felt a stinger in her heart. She tried repeatedly through the years not to think

of that time coming.

She changed the subject, "Did you enjoy the German food, Farah?"

Farah sighed. She knew her mother well enough to know when they were through

talking about something.

"Yes, ma'am. It was delicious. I hope Chance likes his."

Anna giggled and said, "Now you know there are not too many foods your brother

would turn down. He is a growing boy."

When they turned into the driveway, Chance was standing in the door waving at

them, "Mom, I need to speak to you in private please." His brow was creased

showing he was upset.

"Farah go inside and take Chance's food to the dining room. We will be in a minute."

Farah looked mad and said, "I'm old enough to know y'all's secret."

"Farah, I asked you to go inside please," Anna said calmly.

Farah stomped into the house and Anna motioned for Chance to get into the car

with her. Chance said, "Mom, the 2 men were there when I left school after going

over the pictures for the yearbook. I couldn't call you because I left my stupid cell

phone in my backpack that I forgot in my Algebra class."

"Okay Chance, calm down. Tell me exactly what happened."

"I walked out to my truck and parked across from me I saw a black Mercedes. It had tinted windows but the men stepped out of the car and were walking towards

my truck. I put my truck in drive and drove over the lawn at school to get away

from them. One of them had something in his hand. I did not see exactly what it

was. Then I drove around to make sure I lost them and came home and locked

myself in. I don't know where our security was at."

Anna was furious. She told Chance not to worry, that she was going to make a

telephone call and hopefully get all of this stopped. He got out of the car and went

inside. As she dialed Ephriam's private number, she saw the black Mercedes drive

slowly by. Ephraim did not answer the telephone, but there was a message in

Moroccan on the voicemail. Anna calmly said, "Call off your men. They are

terrifying my children and I will not stand for it, Ephraim, or King Ephraim,

whatever you call yourself nowadays. Leave us alone. You made your choice so

many years ago. You broke mine and Chance's hearts so badly, the only decent

thing you can do now is go back to your four wives and live your life. The only

thing I have of yours is your diploma from the university you attended. It was sent

in honor of you post humorous...meaning they thought you were deceased and went ahead and gave you a diploma. You can contact the university and they will

send you a copy. Since all you left me are memories, I will keep the diploma I have

and all of the contents from your apartment and storage shed. Chance found proof

you are alive after all of this time on the internet. I am asking you to call off your

2 men who are following my family and scaring my children."

The voicemail said the message was received and the telephone hung up.

Anna called the security company and they said a female pretending to be Anna

telephoned them and said, their services were not required tonight. Anna asked the

head of the security company to come to her house.

"An imposter canceled your services to night, not me. My son was almost

abducted. Thank God he was not, or I would have sued you. From now on, you and

I will have a password. Before you carry on a conversation with me, or the

children, ask for the password, which will be, <u>currently wise</u>. No one will guess

that to be the password. I now see a need for 24-hour protection for my family. Do

you understand?"

The gentleman looked sick and said, "Ma'am I am so sorry. These people are intelligent and they outfoxed my people tonight. Please forgive me. We will do better."

Anna sighed and said, "I hope so. Please prepare 4 of your men to go on a trip with the children and me. I have to get them away from this stress. We already have our

passports. I need an additional man to drive Chances truck and my car to the

storage facility. You can keep some of your team here to see if the black Mercedes

comes by. I want them to stop them and find out what is going on. I will not have

my children terrorized." "Yes ma'am. I understand. I won't let you down again."

Anna looked at him and shook her head yes. She looked sad. She went inside and

told the children to pack a bag. Anna then called her boss and explained there is a

family emergency and she would not be back for a couple of weeks. She sent an

email message to the school that the children would be out of the country for a

time. She asked that they forward their schoolwork to her and she would make sure

they completed the assignments, then she would email them back to the teachers.

Her boss was very understanding. She was packing her bag when Robert called.

"Hello Anna, it's Robert. How are you?"

"Hello, Robert. I am ...okay. I'm glad you called. I need to go away for a few

weeks. I will explain everything when I get back. I just need to clear my head."

"Anna, are you in danger? Remember I am a Captain with the police department. I can help you." "I just need to go on a mental health vacation with my children,

Robert. I will call you when we land. It's okay really."

Robert didn't sound convinced but said, "Okay, please remember I am here for

you." "Thank you, Robert, that means more than you will ever know."

They hung up and Anna called the housekeeper to let her know she had the next

couple of weeks off with pay. Ultra-tech-savvy Chance used his cell phone to help

purchase the tickets to Madrid, Spain. It was a short time before everyone was

packed and in the security officer's vehicle headed to the airport.

They arrived at the airport just in time to make their flight. Anna had purchased

first class for her and the children and business class for the 4 security officers.

Their trip was from Atlanta, Georgia to Miami, and Miami directly to Spain.

Chance didn't know what his mother was up to but he trusted her completely. He

knew she would never allow Ephriam or anyone to take Farah.

He also knew Spain was one country over from Morocco. The first-class area was

very spacious and luxurious. The children were very impressed with how much

room they had and how good the food was. Anna shook her head and said, "First

class is very expensive, but you guys are worth it. Chance get on your telephone and see if you can find us a Villa to rent for a couple of weeks. It needs to have a

lot of bedrooms. We have the security staff with us."

Chance searched and found a real estate agent that he chatted with. She said, "I

don't have a villa large enough to accommodate that many people, however, I have

a house that has 8 bedrooms, and a pool. It is 15,000 for the month."

Chance told his mother about the offer and showed her pictures of the house. Anna

accepted it. Chance told the agent they would like to rent the house for a month

and Anna would be paying in cash. The agent asked for a deposit, to hold the

house, and Anna sent her cash app $3000.00 to hold the house. Chance told her

they would be there in approximately 5 hours. "We are on the plane, headed your

way."

Anna asked Chance if the landlord could arrange to have groceries brought to stock

up the kitchen so that when they arrived there would be food already there. The

agent said, "We have several women who work as housekeepers and cooks. I could

hire one of each quickly and they will shop for you."

Chance, acting as Anna replied, "That will be fine. Please make sure they are of

good character as I have my children with me and I need to hire high morale and

loyal employees around them."

The agent assured Chance that these women she had in mind were the salt of the

earth types of women, who will treat you like family.

Anna and the children had a peaceful sleep on the airplane. They had never had a

trip this long, but they all did great. 2 cars were waiting for them at the airport. One

for the security team, and one for Anna. The security office in the United States

had arranged for the transportation. The real estate agent met them at the house to

present them with the keys. "Please if you have any issues or need anything, please

let me know."

The house was huge and gorgeous. The security team checked the house before

they let the family enter. Once cleared of any danger, the family entered. They

toured the house and were impressed that people lived that way. Fortunately, there

were 3 bedrooms upstairs and Anna insisted that is where her family would sleep.

The pool was extremely large and beautiful. The housekeeper, Ms. Hussan, and

the cook, Mrs. Rivera introduced themselves. They had already been to the market

and the kitchen was fully stocked.

Anna and the children went to their bedrooms and unpacked. Anna called Robert.

"Hello Robert, we made it safely. I don't know if we will stay 2 weeks or 4. Work has been a bit hectic lately and the children have been restless. I just thought I

should get away."

"As long as you are not running from me," Robert said.

"I'm not running from anything Robert, especially not you. I like you and want to

get to know you so much better. I just need time to think. My job wants me to

move north to take over 10 stores as a General Manager. The promotion would be

great, but I can't uproot my children, I just met you, and there is too much to lose if

I accept the position. They have tried for years to make me take that position, but

now they are placing a lot of pressure on me."

"I'm sorry Anna. I know it's selfish of me, but I don't want to lose what we are

starting. You mean something to me. I think Farah is wonderful and I am certain I

will like Chance when I am given the opportunity."

Anna giggled and said, "He is an amazing son. I am so proud of both of them.

Farah was so thrilled to meet Dorothy. She will be calling her from here, I am sure."

"Are you safe there Anna?"

"Yes, I brought half of my security team on the trip, and the other half is watching

my home. They filed all of the necessary paperwork with your police department."

"Security team? So, there is more to this?"

"Unfortunately, yes there is more, and I will share everything with you later, I promise."

"Okay, just please be safe. Oh, and Anna where are you?"

"We are in Madrid."

"Madrid, Spain?" Robert asked.

Anna laughed and said, "Yes sir."

He whistled then said, "You know how to get away don't you dear?"

Anna said, "I guess I do. Just remember, I am not running. I am regrouping my

thoughts and spending quality time with my children. My head will be on straight

when I get back home, and then you and I can pick back up where we left off if

that is what you want."

"Yes, Anna. That is exactly what I want. I miss you already."

Anna said, "Be safe Robert and I will talk to you soon. You have my number if you

want to talk." And they hung up. Anna didn't put the phone down right away. She

wondered if she were setting herself up for a second heartbreak. Robert seemed so

nice and attentive, but she truly didn't have closure with Ephriam. She had waited

so long for him only to be nearly devastated. She had loved him so much and part

of her died when she received the message that he died. The only thing that kept

her going was her children. Sweet Farah had so many of Ephraim's features and

mannerisms. She wondered if the men following her and her children were trying

to see if she had remarried, or if was she involved with anyone. Maybe the miserable-looking Ephraim decided he couldn't live without her after all of this

time. Anna put her head in her hands. She knew she could never take Ephraim back

for any reason. The deception had been too harsh.

The abandonment hurt Chance so much. No, she couldn't go through that again,

especially since Ephraim had 4 wives. He broke the sacred bond they had, not her.

She wondered if he had wanted the money back that he left behind.

"Too late for that." Anna thought. She had used the money for many things. She

bought a hobby farm for her to run when she retired. She also bought tractors and

other farm equipment that she didn't know how to use. She had the entire farm

fenced in. She had 2 corrals built, one for the horses and one for the miniature

donkeys and goats. There were 2 large chicken condos. A pond was also on the

property as well as a spring-fed well. She had quietly paid for all of the farm with

a little bit of cash at a time. She had even paid the attorney who transferred the

property in her name, in cash. Anna started buying CDs at the bank with a little bit

of cash at a time. She had about 50 CDs. The bank never questioned her and the

CDs were in a safety deposit box. Anna purchased a million-dollar life insurance

policy for herself to go the children should she die. She also purchased 4 storage shed businesses, 6 rental houses and prepaid for Chance and Farah to attend

college. All of this and it had not made a tiny dent in the large pallet of money.

Anna slept fitfully on her first night in Madrid. She was up before the sun.

The children came into her room. They had not slept either. Chance could tell

she had been crying. Farah went to take a shower.

"Mama, why did we come here, so close to where you know who is?"

"I don't know son. I was drawn here to maybe confront him face to face. Maybe I

wanted an apology for him shipwrecking our life for so long. I don't know. I

needed a break from our life. My job is trying to promote me again and I still don't

want it. I am at a crossroads as to what to do. I will not uproot you and your sister.

I am financially able to stop working with the convenience stores. I probably

should do that soon, so they can promote others."

"But Mama, that is the only job you have ever had."

"I know Chance, but I have made some very good investments in other businesses.

I could devote myself to running those."

"Mama, if you choose to meet Ephraim, please make him come here. If you go

there, he could imprison you and we would never see you again."

"I have thought about that son. I don't want him coming here. It would have to be in a public place with our security team in the background watching everything. I

still don't know about it." Chance began to cry, "I don't know why this still affects

me so deeply. I loved him. He is the only father I have ever known. I kept loving

him all of my life, and I waited for him to come back. When you finally

told me he had died, I mourned him like a father. I tried to hide it from you, but I

was angry. I felt cheated out of a life with him. I will be right back mama."

He left the room and returned with photos printed on paper. "I got these pictures

off of the internet mama. These are dated for last week. Look at him.

He looks like he is filled with rage and hatred. He is not the same man. If you tell

him about Farah, we will lose her. She will just be another of his 15 children."

Anna took the papers from Chance. She was horrified to see Ephraim so angry.

She had never seen that side of him when he was with them. These photographs

showed an angry, possibly evil man. Anna hugged Chance and said, "Son, I don't

want you to print any more pictures or read any more articles. The Ephraim we

knew and loved is probably gone. We have to accept that. I don't know when I will

tell Farah the truth. Maybe never. I just don't know. But I do know I will not contact Ephraim unless it is absolutely necessary. I am sure his people know we are

here, which means he knows. It is up to him to contact us."

Chance said, "I smell breakfast. Let's go down and eat."

Anna said, "I will get Farah."

Breakfast was wonderful. The cook spoke English, which helped so much. The

security team took turns eating after the family had breakfast. The housekeeper

made the beds and started dusting the furniture. She explained there was always

dust in the air. She blamed it on the desert of Morocco.

Farah asked, "Mother, can we go shopping and look around Madrid? I think it is a

beautiful place."

Anna answered, "Yes, but we have to stay together no matter what. Madrid could

be dangerous to foreigners if they are not careful."

Farah looked shocked and said, "Then why in the world did you bring us here?"

Anna chuckled and said, "As you said, it is a beautiful place and I wanted you and

your brother to experience it. I have worked too hard, and not provided exciting

adventures to you both. I am trying to make up for that shortcoming. There are

fabulous markets here, museums, art galleries, and all kinds of street dancers.

You may even be able to learn some of the dance routines to take back home and

teach your friends. They also have several drama theaters in English and Spanish.

Chance will be able to photograph anything he sees and give us memories to last a

lifetime. There is only one downfall. You have to do your school work before we

leave the house every day before we head out for adventures."

Both Chance and Farah groaned. "Homework mama? How did they find us?"

Anna smiled and said, "I emailed them and they said they would send the work and

I can email it back to them."

Farah said, "Well I guess I need to buy an alarm clock so I can get it over with."

Chance said, "You can just let the cook know and the smell of that delicious

breakfast will wake us all up."

Anna checked her email. The teachers knew they were away on a family

emergency so they agreed to give a 3-day extension to not give any homework.

They each sent a synopsis of the work the class had done in their absence.

Anna telephoned the head of security back in the United States.

"We will be going into the city as tourists. Please alert your men, so two of them

can go with us to monitor us and keep us safe. The other two can stay here and

make sure no one enters our rented home."

"Yes, ma'am. It is already taken care of. Just so you know, last night my men

installed cameras all around the outside of the home and set up an alarm system on the windows and entrances. If you need the code, just call me. It will be less worry

for you to have to deal with the security code when you have my best 4 men

protecting you and your family."

Anna said, "Thank you. I do appreciate your attention to detail."

The first place they visited was the Museo Museum. Chance was over the moon

with all of the amazing art. They would not allow pictures to be taken, but he did

sneak a few. Anna whispered, "If you get us arrested, you are grounded until you are 30."

Chance laughed and winked at his mother. The afternoon brought a wonderful

meal at a local eatery. It was amazing. They went to the Madrid Zoo. Farah was

impressed with some animals she had never seen before. She begged her brother to

take many pictures. By the time they arrived back at their rented home, all 3 were

exhausted but filled with happiness. The cook had prepared a wonderful meal. She

enjoyed watching them eat. They ate with gusto and enthusiasm.

These were the first Americans she had ever liked, and that was saying a lot

because she had met hundreds of tourists who thought they were better than her.

Not this lot, they were a happy family. The kids even hugged her and thanked her

for a wonderful meal. Madam had raised her children to be good people. Cook

wiped a tear from her eye with her apron.

Chance went upstairs and downloaded his photos to his computer. Farah came into

his room and wanted to see the pictures.

"Sis, I don't know if there is a place to print them off here in Madrid. I just

downloaded them to my computer. But you can look at my camera, just don't

delete anything."

Farah sat on the floor and went through the computer to see the pictures.

"I still can't get over how beautiful the animals were. It was magical."

The next day Anna warned Chance that they were going to the markets for Farah to

shop to her heart's desire. "Son, I have a surprise for you tomorrow so please be

patient and bear with us on the shopping expedition."

They all 3 wore jeans and bright neon green shirts, in case they got separated from

each other. The market was almost overwhelming. The vibrant colors were

phenomenal. Farah found brilliant purple, emerald green, red, yellow, and blue

satin-like fabrics. "Mama I can sew some amazing costumes with this fabric. I

have never seen anything like them. Can you ask them if we can order more to

come to the United States?"

Anna said, "First let's ask the cook if she can send them to us as you need them.

We don't need to be giving out our addresses to strangers." Suddenly Anna saw some gorgeous pottery that was hand thrown. Her heart raced as she told the

children, "Come with me. I see something I want."

Anna picked out about 10 pieces of the pottery for her patio back home. The kids

also picked out some presents for cook and the house keeper.

The cook received a beautiful apron and a gold necklace.

The house keeper received a piece of pottery and a gold bracelet. Both women

were exceptional grateful for the gifts. They each cried and hugged the

children. After the family ate lunch, they each retired to their rooms for a nap. They

were exhausted from the great time they had at the market. That night the family

stayed in for the night. They watched a movie and played one game of Monopoly

which they didn't finish because it was taking too long. Farah decided to sleep with

her mother. Chance sat in his open window, and attempted to take pictures of the

stars. It was about 3 am when he noticed a black Mercedes driving slowly by.

Security did not stop the car and investigate. Chance took a picture of the car, then

yelled out of the window for security, and the car took off. Chance picked up the

telephone and called the head of security. Anna had made sure both of her children

had his number. Immediately Chance could see the car turn their headlights back on. There was a lot of activity in the guard shack, and Anna's security team were

all holding guns and securing the perimeter like they were supposed to be doing all

along. Chance stayed up all night long to make sure there was not a repeat of

dereliction of duties. After they ate breakfast, Chance asked his mother if he could

see her privately. Farah groaned and said, "So we have secrets here too?" and

stormed off to her room. Anna followed Chance to his room and his computer,

Chance orchestrated a Zoom call with the head of security. A zoom call is where

both parties can see each other during the call. His mother asked, Son has

something happened?" Chance said, "Not yet, but something could have happened.

The security team down stairs was not doing their jobs. It was 3 am and a black

Mercedes drove slowly by our house. I saw them stop, and I took a picture of the

car. He showed the picture to his mother and sent it to the head of the security.

Security did not engage the car. As a matter of a fact, I saw both of them smoking,

facing the direction of the house, not the street." Anna clicked the off button on the

computer. She didn't even want to hear any more excuses from the head of

security. She called Ephraim's telephone again. This time someone picked up but did not say anything. Anna spoke calmly. "I have asked you to call off your people

from harassing me and my little family. We are of no consequence to you. What is

in the past, is in the past. You made the choice to abandon us.

Nothing can change the choices you made Ephraim. Can't you see that? We cannot

go back and we cannot start over. Please release me. I have moved on in my mind

and my heart. You have all those wives and children to fill your days and nights. I

am asking as a personal favor, leave us alone."

It completely took Anna by surprise when she heard Ephraim's voice on the line.

"Anna, it's me. Oh my God, I can't believe I am speaking to you. I have missed yo so much. My father's secretary sent you the announcement of the plane crash proclaiming my death. Once it was done and I was told about it, I was devastated. I was told that if I contacted you again, you and Chance would be harmed.

I did not know it, but we were always followed and monitored by my father's men. They were even at the restaurant the night I proposed marriage to you, and you accepted. My father feigned sickness to get me back to Morocco. In his death, I would become King, and I could have changed the rules, allowing you to be my wife and Chance to be my legal Son. My father lived another 10 years, then I took the throne as King. I didn't want it. It had robbed me of my only chance at happiness. A life with you and Chance.

While my father was living, he arranged all of these marriages and demanded I participate in the ceremonies. I do not love one of them. I will have to explain in person. I do not love my children, as I don't know them. Anna, I used up all the love I had in my heart for you and Chance. I just want you to know, there has never been anyone but you in my heart. I could die a happy man, if I could hold you one last time. I want to thank you for all the love you gave me. Chance, my son, how I long to apologize to him.

I know he thinks I abandoned him. He must have been hurt to see pictures of me still alive, while he had spent so long believing I was dead. Anna the laws were different here. I couldn't marry you and bring you here with Chance, unless we said Chance was your brother. I knew you would never accept those terms. I thought if I could reason with my father and make him see how much we loved each other he might help us to be together. I never dreamed he would interfere like he did. I was basically imprisoned here in his castle. I was not allowed to use the telephone, or ever go outside without a security team. I wrote you hundreds of letters. My father saved them and left them unread in a huge box in his office. Is any of this making sense now?"

Anna was crying. "I am so sorry that you had to live like that Ephraim. Is there any way we could meet in public without it being a big scene? I will leave my security people outside if you leave yours. Ephraim was crying too; she could hear it over the telephone. "There is a tiny restaurant in Madrid named Sophia's.

I can be there at 8pm tonight. I will not be dressed as a king. I will have on a white shirt and black pants. Please come. Please bring Chance."

"I will Ephraim but you have to promise me that no one will try to apprehend us or force us to go with you." Ephraim said, "Anna, I swear upon all that is holy. You will not be apprehended only by my thoughts and prayers."

Anna said, "Okay, I will be there at 8pm." And then she hung the telephone up. She called the head of her security and he was very apologetic about last night's incident. "I don't want to fire anyone until you come back to the United States."

Anna said, "I don't want you to fire anyone. I just want my family to be safe. You told me these are some of your best agents. I just think they got complacent and I

don't appreciate it. Okay, I've said my piece. Tonight, I am going to a tiny

restaurant named Sophia's. I am meeting someone. That person will probably have

a security team follow him, but I suspect they will remain outside also so that we

may have privacy. Now this part is very important. My son and daughter will be in

the security car. I want them protected at all cost. We will take 2 separate cars. If

anything happens to me, get them to the airport and call for Captain Robert Ingalls.

He will tell you what to do with my children."

"Yes, ma'am I understand. And again, I am deeply sorry you were not given the

security that you have handsomely paid for."

Anna called Chance and Farah into her room. "We are going out tonight. I have to

meet with someone. We are taking separate security cars in case this doesn't go as I plan."

Farah asked, "Are we in danger?"

Chance spoke up and said, "No. It's just tourist in Spain have to use caution. There

can be bad people everywhere." Then he gave his mother a knowing look.

They all dressed in their best clothes. Anna explained they must stay in the car

unless she came for them.

"I promise we will have a great dinner this evening. But I have to meet with someone first."

Anna and her children arrived in 2 separate cars, at Sophia's restaurant at 7:55 pm.

Anna walked into the restaurant alone. Ephraim was sitting at a table. Noone else

was visible. Both of them burst into tears at the mere sight of each other. They

hugged and Ephraim kissed her forehead, then got on his knees and hugged her

mid-section. Anna let him hold her for a few minutes, then turned loose and sat

down in the chair across from him at the table. He produced a handkerchief to wipe

her tears away. She looked closely at him. He had aged some, but he was still the

man she had lost her heart to so many years ago. He held her hands and said, "You

haven't changed my love. Except you are more beautiful than the first day I lay

eyes on you at the park. Oh my God I can't believe you are here Anna. I'm so

happy to be able to touch you and see your gorgeous face. I want to apologize for having you followed. Ever since, I became King, I kept men watching for you.

Several times they tried to approach Chance to give him a letter from me but it

scared him and he ran away from them. It was never meant to harm either of you,

Anna. I was trying to find a way to reach out to you. You are my only love, always

have been and always will be. I have never stopped loving you for half of a second.

What my father did was cruel and unnecessary, he claimed that was the only way

he thought he could kill our love, by cutting it off at the root. If you thought I was

dead, you and I both would move on with our lives."

Anna said, "Apparently he didn't know the depth of our kind of love."

Ephraim said, "No he didn't. He was cruel. I even offered to abdicate from the

throne but he would not allow it. I suppose that is when he had the announcement

sent to you. He sent me a copy. I wanted to die. For you to think I was dead, I

couldn't handle it. Tell me about your life. life. Tell me about Chance. Did you

adopt a girl. Security keeps talking about a girl that lives with you."

Anna became tense. "Chance is doing great. He is the photographer on his high

school yearbook committee. He is really into taking amazing pictures. He was

the one who discovered you were alive. He was given an assignment in school to

do a research paper on Morocco. He is the one who discovered you are alive.

Ephraim, he suffered so much, not having answers, thinking you dead, then seeing

you look so mad and miserable in the pictures he found on the internet. I think the thing that hurt him the most was seeing all your wives and children." Ephraim bowed his head and said, "Please forgive me Anna. But I would do it all over again, just to have you in my life." Anna sighed, "Ephriam, I cannot compete with 4 wives and multiple children. Whether you love them or not, you are legally bound to them for life. I have accepted that and I want to move on with my life as well."

Ephraim put his head in his hands and wept. Anna went and sat next to him and put her arms around him. His heart was broken, as was hers. When he was finally able to speak, he said, "You never married. You only went on 5 dates for dinner in the time we have been apart. You never invited them back to your house. You must still love me."

"I will always love you Ephraim. However, fate has made sure that we cannot be together as a couple in this life. But we will be friends, best friends for life."

"Yes, I like that. We shall be best friends, until I win you back."

Anna said, "I am going to get Chance out of the car so you can speak to him. He may be reserved, but this is a lot for a 17-year-old to take in."

Ephraim shook his head yes and tried his tears. Anna brought Chance in. Chance broke down and cried. "You were going to be my father, then you faked your death? It doesn't make any sense. We loved you."

Ephraim apologized with all of his heart and explained everything to Chance as best he could. It was very emotional for all 3 of them. "Chance I am still your father no matter what has happened. You have always been my son. I love you."

Suddenly Farah came busting into the room. "How long are you going to keep me in that car mama? Why does Chance get to come in here and not me?" Ephraim looked like he was going to faint. He knew instantly that Farah was his daughter. He looked at Anna and said, "Oh dear God...I didn't know." Anna said, "Neither did I until you were gone."

Ephraim could not contain his tears. Standing before him was his only biological child. She looked like him and acted like her mother. She was beautiful. Anna turned to Farah and said, "Sweetheart, I have something to tell you. This very nice man is your father." Farah was shocked. She sat down on the floor and stared at him. She fought back her tears. Then she said, "You never mentioned him, Mama. I thought you didn't want to talk about it. I never brought it up to you." She looked accusingly at Ephraim and said, "Why are you here now?"

Anna interrupted Farah and said, "I was waiting for the right time to talk to you sweetheart, but the right time never seemed to come. In all fairness your father did not know you existed or I promise you he would have been here long before now." Farah asked, "Is he Chances dad too?" Ephraim spoke up and said, "Yes, yes, I am. I am so happy to meet you, Farah. For many years your mother and Chance thought I was dead. I think your mama was trying to protect you from that awful information. A terrible person sent her the information that I had died. It obviously was a horrible lie. If I had known about you, I would have contacted her sooner, but I did not know. I know this is hard to understand, but your mother and I have decided to be best friends. I hope to come and visit all of you very soon. Are you okay with this?" Farah sat down at the table and looked at Chance. Chance smiled and said, "Sister, it will be okay. Everything is going to be okay now. Our Dad is an honorable man." Farah asked, "What do I call you if you are my father?"

Anna said, "You can call him anything you like."

Farah asked, Can I call you Dad?" Ephraim said, "I would like that very much." He couldn't quit looking at all 3 of them. "I'm so blessed. Here is my little family that I love so much. God is so good." Chance said, "What happened to Allah?" Ephraim smiled and said, "I converted to Christianity years ago son. It is what saved me from losing my mind when I lost you and your mother."

Chance said, "That's awesome dad. I think I am going to start going to church. It just feels like the thing to do."

Their visit was about 3 hours long. Ephraim spent quality time with each of them. Anna produced 2 envelopes.

One was Ephraim's Master's degree from the university he attended. The other was filled with pictures of Chance and Farah as babies and as they grew. Ephraim was thankful for both envelopes. "Anna, I wish you would reconsider marrying me, but I know you won't. At this time, I can't divorce my wives unless they do something against the law or if I figure something else out. I have amends to make everywhere in life, but I assure you that you and my children will never be forgotten or overlooked." Ephraim and Anna walked towards the furthest wall in the restaurant to speak privately. Anna asked him about the multiple children he had back at the castle. He looked down, then said quietly, "Anna, not one of those children are mine. My brother impregnated all 4 of my wives.

I have never had sex with any one of them, ever. My father was insistent that they produce children immediately. My brother knew my heart was here and I got physically sick even thinking about another woman.

When I gave up hope of ever seeing you and Chance again. I took a vow of celibacy. My father was threatening me with all kinds of punishment. My brother knew what state I was in mentally, so he stepped in and secretly did my share of populating. My father never knew and was satisfied. He did not care that I was without love or hope."

"I am so sorry that your life was so difficult Ephraim. Perhaps your father thought you would forget all about us, if he kept you away. Being under house arrest does seem extreme."

"My father was a very extreme man. After 2 years of me being unable to the leave, he told me that you had remarried and therefore forgotten all about me. God forgive me I had begun to hate him. When he finally died, I did not shed a tear. I've been angry ever since. Earlier, he provided people in to counsel me and teach me how to be the next king. I didn't want to be the king. I wanted you and Chance. I wanted to be your husband. I found out after he died that he had you watched since he sent word that I had died in that plane crash. He was making sure we were not communicating in any form. He knew that would have given me hope of a life with you. How did you find out I was alive?"

"Chance was the one who caught on that we were being followed. I thought it was someone trying to take Farah from me. I hired a security team to keep us safe from kidnappers." Ephraim said, "And my father would have tried to steal Farah if he had known about her. She is so beautiful Anna. She looks like both of us. And Chance, Chance is almost a grown man. I am so proud of him. You have done a great job with both of them. I am so ashamed you had to do it all alone. I swear, if things had been different, I would have helped every step of the way. I love you still."

Anna's eyes filled with tears. She said, "They are all I have had in the world since you left. I never quit loving you dear." I went on a couple of dinner dates through the years, but none of them were you."

"I am so sorry. I really believed my father was ill and I had to go check on him. He had not responded to my letter about me wanting to give the position to my brother. I thought he was too sick to respond. He wasn't sick at all. He had just realized I was so in love with you and tricked me into coming back to Morocco. Once I was here, I was basically his prisoner. I could not leave but everything I wanted he had brought to me. I became very depressed. I kept writing those letters to you. My brother is the one who told me my father was having the letters misdirected and delivered to him. He did not read them, he just collected them in a huge box in his office. I found them the day he died. I brought them for you.

All I could think of was, you never knew how much I loved you, and missed you, and that I was alive. Anna, you have to believe, I did not come back to Morocco to be king. I came back to fight for us. Even if I had stayed with you, he would have had me returned to him, if even by force."

"I believe you Ephraim. It all makes sense now. We have gotten older, and our precious children are growing up. Chance is a Senior this year in high school He will be going off to the University next fall. He wants to be a photojournalist. That will leave Farah and I to fend for ourselves. She is very gifted in Drama and she sings like an angel. She is in Choir. She will most likely get scholarships in Drama and Music. Which means she can have her choice of which college she wants to attend." "If any of you need anything, please tell me. I could deny you nothing in this world Anna. You will always be my love. Our children are deep in my heart as well. Will you allow me to come and visit with them."

Anna smiled bravely, but her heart was torn from top to bottom. She said, yes of course, but I don't want Farah to come to Morocco unless she wants to when she is grown up." Ephraim said, "I agree with you. There is always some type of war or threats. I would not want either of my children to come here. Promise me you will not let Chance join the military. There is no honor in dying for a country that doesn't value you."

"Sweetheart, the world is in bad shape right now. Terrorist are wreaking havoc everywhere. I would never encourage Chance to serve in the military." Anna motioned for the children to come over to them. The children hugged Ephraim. He said that he would come in one months' time to visit with them. Farah hugged his neck again and said, "Dad, I look forward to getting to know you." Then Chance hugged him and said, "I look forward to making you proud of me." Ephraim could not hold back his tears. "I already love your mother, and I love each of you children with all of my heart. There is still so much to talk about. I promise I will come next month and we will have a great visit." He asked Anna to read and to sign a paper he produced, she did. As the children walked away, Anna kissed Ephraim on the lips and hugged him. She said, "We will see you soon dear. We are headed back in the morning."

Ephraim touched her face softly and said, "I beg you will call me to let me know you arrive home safe." Anna said, "I will dear." She and the children got in one car and left to go back to the rental house. Chance booked their return trip on his computer. They packed everything and headed home the next morning. Anna decided to keep the security for another month. Anna met with Captain Robert Ingalls for dinner and told him there had been a development in her life and she didn't know if she could commit to him for a while. "Things are complicated. I had a fiancé that I thought was dead, and it turns out he is not. I just need some time to figure this out. He is the father of my children. I have no intention of reuniting with him; however, he needs to get reacquainted with the children and that may take a little time. We have mutually decided to be friends. Do you understand the position I am in here?"

Robert told her, "Anna, I do understand. I will wait for you forever if it takes that long. Do you understand?

Anna smiled and said, "It won't take that long, but I appreciate you saying that. We will still talk every night on the telephone. Don't give up on me Robert?" He kissed her hand and said, "No way."

Ephriam kept his word and arrived at her doorstep in one month. He sent his upset security team to a hotel. He told him he wanted no interruptions, and no sighting of them. They were to keep away from him and Anna and the children. Anna cancelled her security team as well. Ephraim arrived with pounds and pounds of fabric for Farah, and hand forged telescope and cameras for Chance. They were just living on faith and love. Farah and Chance became very attached to Ephriam very quick. It was all very natural and easy. Ephraim was honest with all of them about his wives and how his father had arranged those marriages. He explained how his father sent word to Anna that he had died in an airplane crash, and that he had no knowledge of it for years. He told them about all the letters he wrote to her and Chance, that were never mailed. He brought another big bag of them to give to Anna.Ephraim told Chance how his father had tricked him into thinking that Anna had married. It was very emotional to hear. The children showed off their awards, and things that were special to them. Ephraim was overwhelmed at times because of the wonderful times he had missed in their lives. "Mama always made a video or took pictures when we achieved anything. She documented everything. It was almost embarrassing. If she wasn't taking pictures, Chance was." Farah said with a laugh. After dinner every night they sat thru video after video so that Ephraim could see everything that was documented. One night Ephraim handed Chance an envelope. Chance opened it and his eyes filled with tears. Ephraim had managed to adopt him. Chance asked how did you get mom's signature on this?" Ephraim said, "When we all met in Madrid. I asked her to sign it and she did. She knew you were already my son. This just finalizes it."

Chance laughed then hugged Ephraim, "This is crazy man but I love it and I love you dad." "I love you son. I have since the first day I met you at the park." Farah asked him if he was going to have to adopt her.

Ephraim said, "I already have the paperwork. I just have to talk your mother into signing it." Anna giggled and said, "Of course I will sign it. Now I want you children to get ready for bed. Its late. You have your dad for the next week." The children finally headed to bed. Farah stopped by Chance's room. "It's like a fairy tale isn't it brother? Our entire lives have been turned upside down. It's like a piece was missing and now it makes sense."

Chance said, "Yes, Mom and I kept the secret from you to spare you pain. When I saw on the internet that he was alive, I had such mixed emotions. I was devastated because I had to break it to Mom. I was also devastated because I thought he lied to us. It never occurred to either of us he was kept away from us. We both cried. But Farah, our Dad is a good man and I totally believe his father deceived him for years. He bent him but he did not break him. A lesser man would not have come back to us."

Farah said, "Yes, I think I could love him. But I don't think I ever want to visit Morocco. They might imprison me and never let me see you or Mom again. I do not want that."

Chance said, "Mom would never allow that to happen. I promise you. I have a feeling our dad will be coming here quite often to see us. I can tell he still loves Mom."

Ephraim was talking on the telephone to the head of his security team, so Anna went to say goodnight to the children. She walked in on their conversation. "Is everything okay guys?" "Yes ma'am. Farah was a little concerned about going to Morocco." Anna hugged her and said, "Sweetheart, no one will ever make you go. It is alright now and will remain alright. I promise. Now let's head to bed." She hugged and kissed them both. "Don't forget to say your prayers." Anna said as she went back to the living room. Ephraim was sitting on the couch. They smiled at each other. Ephraim said, "You look exceptionally beautiful tonight, Anna. Is there something special that has you glowing?"

"I'm just so happy to have you here and happy Chance and I could finally share with Farah that you are her father. We hated to not share that with her."

Ephraim said, "I hate it so much that I missed that part of them growing up, but you did document everything so well. I can't tell you how much I appreciate you doing that." He moved a little closer to her and smelled her hair. He always loved to do that when he held her in the past.

Anna sat back and looked at him. He no longer looked like that furious, miserable man in the pictures that Chance found on the internet. His hair had lightened a little bit, and he looked relaxed and happy.

Ephraim asked, "Are you looking for the man I once was? I'm still here, buried under all of this hurt and pain." "I know you are here darling Ephraim. I'm here too. Come with me, I want to show you something."

He followed her into the climate control garage and showed him his furniture she had been saving for years. "Anna! You saved my furniture that I had in storage? I can't believe you did this?" "It was yours and I couldn't let it go. I had this garage sound proofed and climate controlled. The furniture is just like you left in, in great shape. I covered up the large mirror because I couldn't stand to see myself hurting so badly. It is all here. I have used some of the money you left behind to purchase Chance's dream truck and to prepay his college. I also use it to get braces for Farah, and I bought this house, and invested in several businesses. It barely made a dent in the money. I also purchased some CDs at the bank which I used my money from my paycheck to do as to not alert anyone that you left this huge stash of money. In 5 years, I can cash them in and they will be worth more than what I paid for them." Ephraim looked excited as he said, "My love you are so intelligent. I am so proud of you. I left the money for you to use in case something happened to me." "Well, if you remember I had a lot of experience in being poor, and I don't want to experience that ever again. I have tried to make good decisions for the children as well."

"You have done a fantastic job raising our children. I wish to God I could have been here. With all the riches my father had, he would never give me what I wanted more than anything in the world, you and Chance. I went through a dark depression. I didn't eat, couldn't drink, didn't talk. My father actually came to my rooms in the palace to speak to me. He said, 'I hear you are not doing well. Are you sick? Your entire continence has changed over time."

"I told him, you have robbed me of my happiness. I don't want to be the King. I want to go back and marry Anna. Why can't you understand that?"

My father sat down on the floor next to me and said, "Son, duty to one's country is the only thing that matters. You were born to succeed me as king. It is the law of the land. I cannot undo hundreds of years of tradition. It is expected of you. One day you will understand. What I did was for your own good. You will forget the past one day. It will not always hurt." Then he got up and left me sitting there numb. I swore to myself I would never forget the two of you."

Anna hugged him and sobbed. "I slowly took the pictures down about 3monts after I received the telegram that you died in a plane crash. Months later, I found a picture of the three of us under Chances pillow. He prayed for you every night.

When I saw you on those internet pictures, I was stunned. You looked so unhappy, even though you were surrounded by beautiful women and children. I guess I knew then your heart was still with us, her in Georgia. I think that is truly why I took the children to Madrid. I guess it could have backfired. Your security could have overtaken my lousy security and kidnapped us. I wasn't thinking about that. I wanted to see you with my own eyes and part of me wanted you to meet Farah. I wanted you to know your daughter existed."

"I'm so thankful you told me Anna. As I have said before, you, Chance and Farah are my only family. I am a stranger in my own country. The people call me their invisible King. I only attend ceremonies that are absolutely necessary. I do not receive royalty to the palace. I am not receptive to relationships whether professional or personal. I do interact with my brethren's wives or his children.

I have never touched one of them. They are not mine to touch. I begged my brother, when my father arranged the marriages, to stand in for me. The king never attends any wedding. The groom's face is covered so they did not see a face. It was not me. It was Mohamad Alpin, my younger brother. Father never knew. He managed the press so when they announced the marriages and the birth of each child, it was veiled as not a major event. The wives know and were giving then opportunity to vacate with a quite divorce, however they enjoy anything they want, as they are potential Queens.

I have already discussed this with my brother so when I return, I will decree Mohamad Alpin my successor due to my failing health.

There will be a line of doctors to verify. My older brothers have no desire to be King. I will be free to live with you as your legal husband. That is why I have legally adopted Chance and will adopt Farah so they can legally be my children."

Anna looked surprise, "Your health is bad?"

He smiled, "I have lived with a broken heart for 13 years my love, I won't give you up as easy as I give up the throne."

Anna looked relieved and said, "You know Ephraim, lately each night I speak to a man who is falling in love with me. I am fond of him but I know I do not love him. I was waiting to see what happens with you before I decide if I will allow him to pursue me. I am of the belief that our kind of love only comes along once in a lifetime. Tomorrow I will meet with him and discontinue our friendship." Ephraim's eyes widened, "So there is hope for us to be a family?" "Yes, Ephraim, but you have to understand, I do not ever want to go to your country. The politics of that place ruined parts of our life. I harbor deep resentment to it." "I understand my love. You know I have to go back briefly for my exit plan. I pray you will marry me before I leave here. You are wearing my grandmother's ring."

Anna smiled and looked at the beautiful ring on her hand. "I still remember how you surprised me in the restaurant. That was a magical evening." She had to dab her eyes with a tissue. "I don't have enough words to tell you how much I have missed you Ephraim. If I had only known what was happening with you and your father, I would have raised an army to go there and bring you back to me."

Ephraim took her hands into his and kissed them. "You and these children bring me such joy. I love you all so much. Looking at the pictures Chance took from the internet; I don't even recognize myself. I had a furious look on my face, enraged at my father. You have replaced my sadness with joy. I have to go back for a brief time but there will be no fake deaths, no change of plans. I will return to you quickly Anna." Anna spoke up, "You have adopted Chance and are getting the paperwork together to adopt Farah, then we will be married. We will all have your last name. Are you sure you can live here and be happy? As you see there is no palace here, no servants."

Ephraim chuckled and said, "If you remember when we first met, I lived in a tiny apartment and had no servants. I was the servant to your heart. We will figure everything out sweetheart. I promise."

They stood there holding each other, feeling the love that they had felt for each other for years. That evening, Anna met with Robert Ingalls at a local restaurant. Robert said, "My god woman is it possible you get more beautiful every time I see you?"

Anna smiled and said, "You are too kind Robert." The waiter brought him a beer and her a sparkling water. Robert could tell this was their last night together just by the happiness on her face.

"So, I take it you and your children's father are going to work things out." Anna shook her head yes. "I am sorry Robert. I enjoy your friendship so much. I had no idea he would ever come back. I thought he was dead. He is my true love. I want to thank you for being such a good friend. I never meant to hurt you."

Robert looked tired when he said, "In the long run, I just want you to be happy Anna. If he makes you happy, I will step aside. I can't say I'm not disappointed. But the heart wants what the heart wants."

Anna said, "I'm sorry Robert, my children are so happy."

She stood up and hugged Robert's neck. "If he lets you down, I will be here."

Anna smiled and said, "Goodbye Robert. Thank you."

It hurt his heart to see her walk away. He flagged the waiter and ordered a bourbon on the rocks. He sat there and drank in silence. He only had one drink, 7 times.

Ephraim ordered dinner for him and the children. They were sitting on the floor eating and enjoying each other's company. Chance said, "Dad, I will be going off to college soon. I almost didn't go because I didn't want to leave mama. She's been so strong for all of us. I'm so thankful you will be here with her and Farah." "You know son, I asked you to be the man of the house until I returned. You have done a fantastic job. Thank you for taking such good care of your mama. I am so proud of you."

Farah spoke up, "Okay, all of this emotional speaking is going to have to stop. Dad I'm glad you are here, but you, mom and Chance burst into tears every time you guy's talk is making me crazy. Can we please have a no cry area?"

Ephraim and Chance laughed. "You are right daughter. Even though these have been mainly happy tears. It's time for laughter and happiness."

Anna came in and said, "Hello family!" They all said, hello at the same time. "I am going to change clothes then I will come back out here. I hope yall saved me some food. I'm starving." "Of course we did sweetheart. "Ephraim said with a smile. He loved her and her southern accent." Anna met with her General Manager and resigned her position. It was time to let it go. She was not going to accept the job up north; she had other businesses that needed her attention and of course her family. The company President was sad to see her leave after so many years, but understood she had a life to start living.

Ephraim did go back to Morocco for 4 days. He flew right back to his family. He and Anna were married by the Justice of the Peace, with Chance and Farah as their witnesses. He did not regret abdicating the throne. He never wanted to be a king. His brother was thrilled to be king. War was always looming and he saw his father lose too much sleep over political decisions. Chance went to college and became a photojournalist as he had planned. He graduated with honors. To her surprise, Anna got pregnant and Ephraim was able to participate in this pregnancy. At first, she felt she was too old, but Ephraim was so excited and happy. He calmed her fears and went to every doctor's appointment with her. Nine months later, they had a little boy they named, Raymond Omar. Farah graduated college and became an

Optometrist. Eventually she had a very successful practice. Chance loved traveling for assignments and was acknowledged with a Pulitzer Prize for his documented work in Africa. Ephraim and Anna moved to the Hobby Farm, and learned to work the land. They enjoyed taking care of the animals, tending the gardens and attending a small country church. Farah and her brother Chance married their college sweethearts. Ephraim made sure both of their weddings were exquisite. He was best man at Chance's wedding and he gave Farah away to her husband at the altar. The children continued to stay close to their parents. Anna and Ephraim raised their youngest son, and worked the businesses they owned. Raymond was very athletic as he grew. Raymond played every kind of sport. Ephraim was very proud of all of his children. In his high school years Raymond was scouted by football teams and received many scholarships. He chose to attend Auburn University in Auburn Alabama. It was only 1 ½ hours away from home. Raymond was drafted in his junior year and played for the Atlanta Falcons. Raymond played professionally for 5 years then quit to return to college. He graduated with top honors and became a veterinarian. Anna, Chance and Raymond gave Ephraim and Anna 7 grandchildren. Those grandchildren were the lights in their eyes. Life is good when you are where you are supposed to be and with whom you are destined to be with. The couple retired at 70 and traded in their Hobby Farm for a condominium. They lived their lives happily together.

Anna died of natural causes at the age of 83, Ephraim died 3 days later. The doctor said they could find nothing wrong with Ephraim and said he died of natural causes. One just refused to live without the other for a second time.

The End.

Also by Lilly Buchanan

Bad girls
Rahab

King Marc 1
King Marc

Life in a small town
New Life in a Small Town

Standalone
Our Second Chance
Dannie
Leroy
Sugah
The Wright House
Jezebel 2
Kitty's
Murder in Potluch

Writer
A Mother's Love
Ten Short Stories

About the Author

Lilly Buchanan is originally from Columbus, Georgia. She currently lives in Pascagoula, Mississippi. Lilly started writing when she was a little girl. Lilly loves pretty things, flowers, decorating, writing beautiful stories, volunteering and Jesus! Lilly has 2 amazing granddaughters, Jasmine and Alexandria. If you stop and ask she will show you pictures!!

About the Publisher

Self publishing with Draft to Digital has been an amazing experience.

www.ingramcontent.com/pod-product-compliance
Lightning Source LLC
Chambersburg PA
CBHW031124160726

47989CB00016B/998